I0628531

DIVIDED HEART

QUEENS OF KINGS (BOOK 2)

LAQUETTE

DIVIDED HEART

QUEENS OF KINGS (BOOK 2)

LAQUETTE

Divided Heart
Copyright © 2015 by LaQuette All Rights Reserved
Published by: Brooklyn Girl Ink, LLC

No part of this literary work may be replicated conveyed in any form, by any methods,
electronic or mechanical, including photocopying, recording, or by any data storage
and recovery system without expressed written permission by the Publisher except
where permitted by law.

Photo Credit: CURAphotography via dollarphotoclub.com

Cover created by Taria Reed

Edited by: Elizabeth A. Lance

Disclaimer:
This is a work of fiction, any similarity to actual persons living or dead, products,
businesses and locations are purely coincidental or used in a fictional manner.
This work of fiction contains adult content: depictions of sexual acts, explicit language
that may be objectionable by some readers. This work is intended for adult audiences of
18 and older. Reader discretion is advised.

DEDICATION

For my readers...because you rock!
For Faith H. because you believe even when I don't.

ACKNOWLEDGMENTS

To God, from whom all blessings flow, thank you for the gift, the desire, the support, and the opportunity. To Damon, this does not happen without you. Love you forever. To Sterling and Semaj, my heartbeats, the best parts of me. To my family and friends, thank you for putting up with my craziness. To the Sarah and Hot Ink Press, thank you for the opportunity and the support. To Piper Kay, I will never be able to thank you for making me, "Push the fucking button." To Elizabeth, thank you for making my crazy sound amazing. To Lexie, thank you for supplying me with my new motto, "Hustle until you don't have to introduce yourself" (unknown). To all my JMC and LIJ people, your love strengthens me. To my Loungers, you guys hold me down and keep me going. Thank you so much for the loyalty and encouragement. To the readers, you will never know how much I appreciate your support. Thank you for taking this journey with me.

Keep it sexy,
    LaQuette 💋

COPYRIGHT ACKNOWLEDGMENTS

The following pieces of musical art were mentioned in this book.
Ride by Ciara feat Ludacris
Original Release Date: April 26, 2010
Release Date: April 23, 2010
Label: LaFace Records

Na Na by Trey Songz
Original Release Date: January 21, 2014
Release Date: January 21, 2014
Label: Atlantic Records
Copyright: 2014 Atlantic Recording Corporation for the United
States and WEA
International Inc. for the world outside of the United States. A
Warner Music Group
Company

Grind on Me by Pretty Ricky
Original Release Date: May 17, 2005
Release Date: May 17, 2005

Label: Atlantic Records
Copyright: 2005 Atlantic Recording Corporation for the United States and WEA International Inc. for the world outside of the United States

Divided Heart
Queens of Kings (Book 2)

She broke his heart…to rebuild his soul.

The last two years of Heart MacKenzie Searlington's life have been a constant forward motion of change. She's been promoted to NYPD captain of the seventy-fourth precinct in Brooklyn, a job she never wanted, but is slowly finding her way through with the help of a dedicated second in command and a house full of exemplary officers.

Married to the sexy and powerful mogul, Kenneth Searlington, Heart is living all of the dreams she never knew to ask for before she fell in love with the man that stole her heart. Although Kenneth bathes her in his love and devotion, insecurities from the past still haunt her and cast a dark veil over their union.

Kenneth Searlington knows only one thing, he worships his wife. He has a singular purpose: to love her as hard as he can for the rest of their lives and to neutralize any threat that dares to come up against them. But how does he protect them when that threat comes from the woman he loves?

Thrown by a devastating loss, Heart allows pain and despair to drive a wedge so large between them they may never be able to recover. Pushed beyond his limits, excluded and taken for granted, Kenneth has to decide whether to allow darker urges to control him, or to use his rage to fight for the one thing he adores, Heart.

Can they mend the rift, or will a divided heart end their legendary love?

PROLOGUE

*H*eart Searlington couldn't think around the loud pounding of her own charging heartbeat in her ears. She tried to shake her head clear, but the large fingers wrapped around her throat bit further into the sensitive flesh of her neck restricting her air a little more than she was comfortable with. She just needed a second and she could turn this situation around. If she could just...who the hell was she fooling? She couldn't break free, not the way her aggressor had her pressed into the hard wall, wood splinters piercing the skin of her back like tiny daggers.

She'd never seen him this way, he'd never handled her this way, but then again she'd never given him reason to touch her this way before. That thought caused a hard shudder to pass through her. The realization that she'd caused this, she'd turned him into this raging beast that stood before her, eyes wide with fire, the muscles of his face pulled taut, arm locked with his hand fastened around her throat in rage.

She didn't recognize this man and that above all else scared the living fuck out of her. This man could hurt her, this man could end her. As a captain in the NYPD, she knew how to protect herself against assault, but even her training wouldn't help her now. With the anger staring back into her eyes she knew there was nothing she could do to overpower him.

Her brain fought through the building fogginess that seemed to get thicker with each of her labored breaths. Was he really squeezing hard enough to restrict her airflow? No, more likely it was due to the heaving panicked breaths she was taking through her mouth. He hadn't hurt her yet, but the way he was holding her so roughly, the way his ire radiated off of him, filling the air and chocking her, made her flight or fight response kick in.

She struggled against him, clawed at the arm locked stiffly in place, but she couldn't move it, couldn't dislodge it.

My God, he could kill me.

She saw his lips begin to move. He was speaking, she needed to focus, whatever he was saying could determine whether they both survived this incident or not. Because if he harmed her, the NYPD and her family would hunt him down to the gates of hell and she couldn't allow that to happen.

She'd done this; she'd made him this thing that was holding her so harshly. She couldn't let him suffer another loss. She'd taken so much from him; she'd not take the freedom, the life, and soul he would surely lose if he brought physical harm to her. "Kenneth...please... don't," she mouthed.

"What was that?" Kenneth said as he pressed closer. "You're still trying to control this situation, Heart? When are you going to get it? Your life is quite literally in my hands."

She tried to take another breath, hoping to talk him down, but he shook his head and made a soft shushing sound.

He drew back his free arm and she struggled frantically to get away, her body cringing, preparing for the blow. She closed her eyes, not wanting to see this moment happen, not wanting the memory of this violent moment imprinted on her brain, not wanting to remember the fear that was vibrating through every cell of her body.

He brought his hand down hard against the wall next to her head, the force shaking the hanging pictures and knocking them to the floor beside them. She jumped, but his strong grip held her fast, not allowing even the smallest of movements.

Please don't do this, please don't...

"I've listened too long to what you've had to say. No, today, we're going to do things a little differently. I'm going to talk and you're going to listen. You will never disrespect me like that again. You will never take my kindness as a sign of weakness again. You will learn that just because I don't go around thumping my chest and beating the shit out of you every chance I get, doesn't mean that I am to be fucked with. I'm a lot of things, Heart. But weak has never been one of them. You'd do best to remember that shit.

"I've spent the last fourteen weeks in a hell I couldn't have imagined if I'd tried, because you forced me to make a decision that you knew would destroy us. I had my world ripped out from under me, everything taken from me all because things had to be your way or no way. Well

I've lost everything, Heart, but the one thing I'm not about to lose is you."

He snatched his hand away from her neck just as quickly as he'd placed it there in the first place and turned to walk to the opposite wall. As soon as he'd released her she felt her legs give and her back slide down the wall until she was seated on the floor.

She took a shaky hand to her neck and allowed her fingers to quickly run across sweat-laden skin. She was fine, she'd be fine, but Kenneth...

She watched him rake hard, angry fingers through the dark waves of silky black hair. Her fingers twitched a bit, they ached to feel those soft tresses caressing aching skin. She wanted to go to him, hold him, make things right, the way she should have three months ago, but she knew it was too late, nothing she did would fix the hurt that she'd heaped on his broad shoulders.

"This bullshit with you running behind these fucking emotional mountains you've erected, hiding from me, that shit ends now. I am your husband, and there isn't an inch of this Earth I wouldn't cross to get to you. You can be mad with me, but the one thing you will never do is end us, Heart. The sooner you figure that shit out, the better off we'll both be. Like it or not...You.

Are. Mine."

She might not have liked what he was saying. She damn sure hadn't liked the way he'd expressed it, but she knew one thing...he was right, she did belong to him.

CHAPTER 1

*S*ix months earlier...

*C*aptain Heart Searlington took the familiar right turn onto Essex Ave from Linden Boulevard. She sailed down Essex at a comfortable speed and arrived at her destination in a few short moments. She slowed her dark blue sedan and slowly made the turn into the parking lot of her house, the seventy-fourth precinct in Brooklyn, New York.

She inched slowly into the parking lot preparing to turn into her reserved captain's spot as soon as she saw the opening. She stopped the car in the exact place that she usually did, flicked her right indicator on and prepared to cut her steering wheel to the right. Just as soon as the car inched forward she slammed on the brakes when the rear end of a silver luxury sedan came into her view.

Sitting boldly in her reserved spot was the very same car that had been sitting in her lieutenant's spot two years ago. That car, or rather its owner had changed her life and she wondered what on Earth would warrant a visit at this hour of the morning from the owner.

She thought back over the last two years and the journey she'd taken to get to this place, to the happiness that rested securely in the recesses of her heart. She'd walked into her precinct two years ago and been handed a kidnapping case by her then captain, David Porter. She'd fought it, she'd beasted at Porter for trying to stick her with a case like this and he'd told her in no uncertain terms that he was top cop in the house and that she was going to do as she was told.

The truth was, Porter really should have choked her out for the way she'd spoken to him.

Instead, he'd put her in her place, handed her the case file, and sent her on her way to meet the uncle of the abducted girl. And that's when things changed for her.

Kenneth Searlington, uncle to Merridith Searlington Grant, walked into her office all cocksure and confidence with his money, designer clothes, long hair, and relentless good looks and proceeded to turn her very regimented world upside down. Damn, the truth was Kenneth had tilted her world on its axis and spun that son of bitch like a toy top. By the time the spinning had come to an end she was wobbly, shaky legs unable to hold her weight, questioning what the hell had happened to her, and wondering how she'd managed to fall in love with the man.

She laughed to herself as she shook her head. Hell, falling in love with Kenneth hadn't even been the craziest development in their personal melodrama. No, she'd fallen for the man, and gone and married him too.

She ran her thumb across the ridiculously large blue diamond engagement ring Kenneth had seated on her finger two years ago. It was a habit she had anytime she was thinking about her tycoon husband.

A horn blowing behind her pulled her from her pleasant memories, and forced her to deal with her situation at hand. Out of a parking spot, she pulled her car into the no parking grid and made her way inside her house.

Her house.

She loved the sound of that, reveled in the rhythmic movement of the syllables that made up those two very simple but amazing words. She'd dedicated more than a decade to the seventyfourth and now she was the captain of this precinct that had served as a lifeline for her over the years. She'd give her life for this house, had almost done so on a couple of occasions, so landing a captain's spot here was a perfect dream come true for her.

She pulled her gear out of her car and headed into the station. The squad room was abuzz with its usual noises. Phones ringing, computer keys clicking, voices carrying, the noisy heavy bars of the sliding holding cell door—just the usual.

She passed through the squad room quickly nodding her head to the various greetings her staff members lobbed at her. She'd made it all the way to her office and twisted the knob, anticipation of what she would find making her palms itch. When she pushed the door open she found what she was looking for.

He was a tall man with alabaster skin and midnight locks that fell beyond his shoulders and down his back. He was dressed in a crisp grey business suit that made his crystal blue eyes sparkle. He wore a knowing smile that said, "I know you know that I'm the shit." He was a cocky bastard, true, but she had firsthand knowledge of just how amazing he really was. She also had firsthand knowledge that everything that self-assured smile promised, he was more than capable of delivering. He sat on her desk with his long legs stretched out in front of him and crossed at the ankles. Easy, calm, confident, and sexy as all fucking hell.

"You know you're risking life and limb by sitting on my desk like you own it, right?" she asked as she closed the door behind her. She looked around to make certain the blinds on her office windows and doors were in a closed position, this was a moment that was meant solely for the two of them.

"I may not own the desk, but I own the woman that it belongs to… so I kinda do own it if you think about it," he said as the silky sureness of his voice traveled across the room and pulled her to him.

Before she could say just how it happened, she was standing in front of him between spread legs, falling into the broad expanse of his chest. "You own me do you?" Her voice hitched as she felt his fingers skate from her fingers to her arms causing her skin to sizzle.

"I thought that's what these rings we wear meant? I own you, you own me? Was I wrong?" He leaned in and placed a light kiss on her cheek, and just like any other time his skin met hers, a sensual burn began to singe the area where his lips had rested for only a brief second.

"Mmmm," she moaned. "You bet your pretty ass we belong to each other." She wrapped her hand in his long tresses and pulled him to her, letting her body sink into his and searching for the connection only his kiss could bring. She found his warm, soft lips and mewled into the decadence of the pleasure they ignited inside her.

"God I wish we were home instead of in my office," she said when they broke apart, lungs burning from lack of air. She dove in for one more kiss and then leaned back to look into those hypnotic blue eyes of his. "When did you get back, Kenneth? I thought you weren't coming home for another three days."

With Kenneth being gone for the last week on a business trip, she'd only spoken to her husband via video chat and stolen moments through text messages. To have him here, this close to her, close enough to smell and taste... She was just this side of tempted to say to hell with the workday and go home and sex her man until they were both too exhausted to do anything but sleep.

"That was the original plan, but I needed my wife, missed you too much. I don't think I slept more than a couple of hours at a time, needed you next to me. Not to mention I was a growly beast because I missed you so much. I think the team worked triple time just to get me home to you and out of their hair."

She smiled at him, always happy to know he was just as addicted to her as she was him.

"I'm glad you stopped by, I missed you too. I know you've been on the other side of the world, but over here, it's the start of the work day."

"Come on," he wined, pouting his bottom lip out like a petulant child. "You're the boss, can't you play hooky today, Captain Searlington?"

She shook her head. "Not today. I have a meeting with the inspector in a few hours. I need to prep for it. I may be top cop in this house, but I still have bosses."

He pulled her to him and nuzzled the exposed skin of her neck. "What time do you think you'll be home?"

"As long as brass doesn't lay anything too heavy on me at this meeting, it should be a regular day. I can probably be home by five or six."

Kenneth groaned. "You can't do any better than that? I haven't seen my wife in over a week."

"Go home and go to sleep," she said softly as she let her hand slide over the broad expanse of his chest. "Be ready for me when I get home. I promise I will show you just how much I missed you."

"Mmm, see that right there…" he kissed her lightly on the lips, "…Captain Searlington…" he nipped her bottom lip with his teeth, "…is exactly why I love you."

She went to lean in for another kiss; her forward motion was halted by a soft tapping on the front office door. She stepped out of her husband's embrace, wiped her lips and smoothed her clothes. No need giving her subordinates a show they didn't need to see. When she was certain she looked the part of the respectable leader she said, "Come in," to whoever was on the other side of the door.

"Cap'n," Detective Timothy Grazzo peeked his head inside of the door. "Lieutenant Smyth has set us up in the conference room, he asked that you join us, ma'am."

Heart rolled her eyes. When she'd met Timothy Grazzo two years ago, it had been under the alias of Mancino Forze. Forze was a rooky cop with a bad attitude who liked to piss off his superiors. When she'd first met him she believed him to be a racist prick with a badge that she'd wanted out of her command. Later she discovered he was a veteran detective working undercover for Internal Affairs to find out who set her up to get shot two years ago.

"Grazzo, you like working here right?" He nodded his answer quickly.

"Lose the ma'am or I'm signing transfer papers for you ASAP."

His eyes widened slightly and she could see the hint of contemplation behind those onyx eyes of his.

"Try me if you want to," she said, her smile inching up as she spoke.

He nodded and returned her smile. "Yeah, Cap'n."

Grazzo closed the door behind him. She turned to Kenneth and gave him a quick peck on the cheek. "I gotta go be captain now. See you at home."

"Indeed you will."

~

*H*eart walked into the conference room where her detectives were assembled. Well, technically they were Bryan's detectives now. Yes, she was top cop in the house. She handled all of the administrative dealings of the precinct, and she made all executive decisions regarding policy and how the house functioned. But command was Bryan's as it had been hers when she wore the lieutenant's shield.

She eased into the room and sat on the side, with them, but not really, that seemed to be the constant position she played in her new role of captain. She sat back and watched as Bryan moderated their case breakdown.

He was good; she'd known he would be. Bryan hadn't wanted leadership, but he'd been cast into the role when Heart was promoted. It had taken her forever to convince the man to even apply for the damn position; he fought against change so desperately. But standing at the head of the table, leading his team, command looked good on him.

His detectives, Jenson, Thomas, Ramirez, Santini, and newcomer, Grazzo, all tuned in to receive the pertinent details of the case. "That stretch of after dark desolation from Pitkin and Williams Aves all the way down to Pitkin and Van Sinderen Aves is what the community affectionately calls Ho Stroll. It's a block of industrial buildings there. Once everything closes down, the freaks come out at night, and if you're paid, you can play," Bryan said to the room. Everyone present was familiar with the area and the criminal element that ran rampant through it.

"In the last two months we've seen an increase in criminal activity, especially murder," Bryan continued. "In two months we have three dead prostitutes. Damia Grey, Blanca Fernando, and Emily Silverson were all killed within four weeks of each other. They were all killed by some method of strangulation, all sex workers in that area, all found with the same kind of ligature marks on their wrists, ankles and throat, all with their breasts mutilated, and all posed with their hands in the same angel-like formation across their chests."

Ada Ramirez, the only other female in the room raised an auburn eyebrow as she interjected.

"Lieutenant Smyth, are you trying to say we have a serial killer in fucking Brownsville,

Brooklyn?"

Just hearing those two words in the air associated with their jurisdiction felt like frigid water sliding down the grooves of her spine. The area in question was flanked by the overhead L train tracks on one side and the Remeeder Projects on the other. The area had one of the highest crime rates in their jurisdiction and adding the possibility of something this explosive to the pot just made her twitch with uneasiness.

She lifted her eyes and met Bryan's equally concerned gaze and nodded just slightly, giving him permission to proceed.

Bryan shoved both hands in his pockets and turned to answer Ramirez. "We don't know. But the fact that this is the third killing with four weeks separating each of the murders has us cautiously concerned. Technically speaking, so far, these murders meet all of the criteria necessary to categorize this person as a serial killer. But before we jump to that conclusion, we want a little more information. That's why we sent info to the FBI and once we hear back from them we'll know how we should proceed with this."

Ramirez nodded her head and picked up her pen and pad, poised to write, setting off an identical chain reaction in the other detectives seated around the table. "So what do you have for us L.T.?" Ramirez asked.

"We need to play this one close to the vest. We don't want to panic the public unnecessarily. Right now we're going to investigate and gather as much evidence as we can. I've already sent the case files to the Feds; hopefully they'll have something for us soon. Until then, don't mention the phrase 'serial killer' to anyone."

They all nodded and looked to Bryan for further instruction. He stepped aside giving Heart the floor.

It was so strange how things had changed. It used to be her leading these meetings, her handing the floor over to her captain after she'd prepared her people. Now that was Bryan's job and she was top cop to a precinct that might have a serial killer running around in its streets.

What the fuck was I thinking when I took this damn job?

"I'm headed to One Police Plaza in a bit to go see brass about the case," Heart said.

She watched as all their faces took on a little surprise mixed with a little inquisition, and suspicion. It was how she'd trained them, how she'd taught them to piece information together to work a case.

Sage Santini ran a hand through his dark wavy locks and sat up a little straighter in his chair.

"Why is One Police Plaza calling you in already, Cap? We've just started?"

She nodded; she'd known they'd pick up on it. Her detectives were good; there wasn't much that could be hidden from them.

"You're right; they usually wouldn't be calling me this soon for a face to face. Except, this situation is a little bit different than most."

Santini let a cynical huff push through his lips. "Please don't tell me the fat cats up there in the city suddenly give a fuck about murder in Brooklyn."

She shook her head, she knew she couldn't lie; she had no intention of even trying.

The streets of areas in Brooklyn like East New York and Brownsville held consistently high crime rates. Those neighborhoods fell below the poverty line making them perfect breeding grounds for criminal activity. As long as the only people hurt were the people that lived there, brass didn't really give a damn.

That was the part of her job she hated, the fact that there was such a huge class and financial divide. Those gaps often affected how she could protect the citizens of her jurisdiction. Cutbacks in overtime and resources minimized her ability to drum up manpower and work cases quickly and efficiently. The only time NYPD brass cared about shit like this with such swiftness was when someone with notoriety and privilege was involved.

"This guy is killing prostitutes. Except, one of the girls wasn't a prostitute, she was an aide to the sitting governor," she leaned over the table and tapped a pointed finger on the tip of the picture in the center, then pulled an enlarged copy of a Driver's License photograph. "Emily Silverson is or was one of the governor's top aides. We need to know why she was even in this area to begin with. Was that intentional or just coincidence? That being said, top dogs are going to be all over me about this, which means I'm going to be all over Smyth and he's going to be all over you. Do what you do, and find this son of a bitch quick. Otherwise, there's going to be a mountain of headaches for all of us."

CHAPTER 2

*K*enneth woke to a pounding ache between his legs. He stretched, trying to get comfortable, but the skin on his raging hard on just pulled tighter, making him wince with pain. He pushed his hand between his legs and palmed his cock in a slow gentle squeeze. Afraid that too much of a grip would send him spilling into his own hand, he opened one eye and looked at the clock on his nightstand.

"Seven at night, where the hell is my wife?" Kenneth growled. He tried to turn over, but the pulsing, rigid length between his legs just throbbed harder at the threat of motion. "Arrgghh." He closed his eyes and pressed a hand against himself again hoping to counter the ache when he felt a recognizable tingle dance down his spine.

The edges of his mouth inched up and pulled pink lips into a relieved smile. She was home, or at least near. He didn't need to see or hear his wife because he always felt her. It didn't matter where they were, or how far apart they were, whenever they were near each other he always felt her. It was like she was in his blood, whenever she was close to him; his body physically reacted, pulled him to her.

"Need you," was all he said as he gingerly slipped loose fingers around his angry cock edging himself closer to the hungry release his body needed. His heart rate crept up and his breathing became ragged with anticipation. He felt his side of the bed dip and he took a deep breath...waiting for the singe of her touch against already burning skin.

Soft but sure fingers made a slow trail from his ankle, up his leg, to the inside of his thigh. They stopped there momentarily, hovering so close to where he needed them to be. The agonizing pause ended and he felt those digits that had spent so much time learning his body over the last two years surround his cock making him hiss through clenched teeth.

"I come in from a grueling day of work and you expect me to work some more?" Heart asked with simmering heat scorching the contours of her voice.

He opened hooded eyes just enough to glimpse at her. He could see the slight tinge of red just beneath her skin that always signaled her desire for him. She burned with it, inside and out and that shit just turned him on.

His aching flesh still cradled in her hand burned with need. He quickly snaked out a firm hand around the back of her neck and yanked her down to him leaving their lips just a breath apart.

"You're damn right," he growled out between clamped teeth and locked jaw.

He pressed unyielding lips to hers and forced his way into her mouth. He pulled her body flush over his and turned her into the plush bedding. He maneuvered a leg between hers and used one hand to secure her hands over her head. He sought out the sensitive line of her neck and buried himself there, teeth grazing over the heated flesh.

His tongue slide over her pulse and he moaned in appreciation of that familiar mix of heat and freshness that always greeted him wherever his mouth landed on her body. He found his way back to her mouth, tongue plunging, battling, devouring and she surrendered to ever bit of it without hesitation. They'd come to that unspoken agreement from the very beginning. Out in the world she was Captain Heart Searlington. In here—in this bed she was *his* wife and *his* rule was the only rule.

And rule number one in this room was that neither of them ever came to bed dressed in anything that couldn't be easily pushed aside or removed. When he wanted his wife, which was pretty much every hour of the day, he didn't want to have to rest garments to get to what was his. Without hesitation, he ripped the blouse she was wearing until it rent in two tattered halves exposing creamy sorrel-brown skin.

"Damn, Kenneth," she huffed out. "I liked that damn shirt."

"Then you should have taken it off before you came to bed. You'd better be glad you're wearing a skirt today, or I'd rip that off too."

He roughly pushed up the material of the pencil skirt she was wearing and pulled at the thin layer of silk and lace covering her mound. He heard the sharp sound of her panties ripping and his sex ached just a little bit more.

He slid his fingers between her satin folds and was greeted with fiery moisture. He sank two fingers slowly inside of her opening and they both gave a slow moan of satisfaction. He scissored his fingers, stretching her, the pads of his finger searching for the bump of nerves seated at the top front wall of her canal. When his fingers grazed over it she gave him a rewarding snap of her hips.

He stayed there, applying fast and sharp strokes to what he affectionately termed her kill switch. Her body rippled with pleasure and her voice hitched higher as she sobbed in titillation. God those sounds... They were raw, and powerful, and so open that he could feel his balls inching closer to his body. He pressed in three more strokes and with a sharp flick of his wrist she was screaming in earnest, her walls clamping down on his fingers and her juices skeeting out across his hand, forearm and bed.

The sight of his woman squirting... Each contraction of her womb rewarding him with a powerful gush of her arousal almost made him lose his shit right there without having to place the slightest touch on his cock. He took a slow controlled breath, trying diligently to reign himself in. He'd waited a week to fall into her depths and he wasn't about to miss out by spilling his seed on her thigh like some schoolboy.

Before her body could come down from the powerful orgasm, he pressed her thighs in an open position and pushed the length of his unsheathed cock from head to root inside her. In one swift and certain movement they were joined.

He didn't pause, didn't give them time to adjust, he instantly set up a punishing pace that kept them both moaning. Her velvet fire surrounding him like a tailor made sheath whose delicious friction made the weighted balls in his sack feel like rocks.

He bent down, pressing a harsh kiss against her lips, swallowing the groans of pleasure that escaped between them. He flipped her over onto her stomach and placed a firm grip on her hips and pulled her onto all fours. When she was perfectly posed on both arms and legs, he pressed between her shoulder blades shoving her face into the pillow she was nearly shredding between fiercely clasped fingers.

"Don't. Fucking. Move," he ground out in sharp tones.

He pushed back inside of her and found immovable purchase with his hands on her shoulder, bent leg, and a planted foot. He snapped his hips, and forced her back onto him in the most exquisite slide and his dick plumped up just a bit more, his skin burning with the stretch his current state of erection was causing him.

He pushed and pulled, balls slapping against the opening of her cunt, covered in her slick, causing fire to climb from his sack to his spine, traveling to his blood, burning every nerve ending. This was going to end soon.

He bent down, his front covering her back and reached around, pressing fingers against the swollen pearl of her clit. She tightened around him as his fingers applied pressure. Her muscles spasmed uncontrollably locking around him. He stroked her again and she clamped all of her muscles down in one single contraction as she yelled her completion into the pillow beneath her face.

Satisfied with her climax, he focused on his own and he drove into her over and over until he felt the pins and needles of muscle exhaustion crawling from his toes up the twitching muscles in his thighs. Molten fire erupted from the tip of his cockhead and his muscles let go of everything he'd been holding in for the past week. He sounded his pleasure into the air with a long guttural howl. As he pulsed spurts of his cum into her, he collapsed against her back and bit down onto her shoulder as the endless orgasm kept him in fixed stasis.

When he could manage some sort of control over his limbs he fell over onto his back and pulled his wife into his arms. As great as their lovemaking was—and it was always great—the quiet intimacy they shared, the easy mutual connection between them, that was what he couldn't do without. The knowledge that he could be completely bare with her made their marriage essential to him.

Kenneth knew from years of working and living in the cutthroat world of high society that placing your vulnerabilities on display was the easiest way to destruction. Weaknesses were for exploitation, for decimation. But with Heart...the moments where his soul was stripped raw in front of her, those were the moments where he'd known an unimaginable bliss.

He tugged her closer, relishing in the sparks of lust and love that burned in slow embers along the surface of his skin. "I missed you," he said.

She snuggled closer, skirting her fingertips across his skin, her ear pressed to his chest directly over his heart.

"You mean you missed this," she said waving a finger back and forth between them.

"Yeah, I did miss this, I always miss this, but I missed you even more than this."

She lifted her head and braced her chin across stacked hands on his chest. "Careful there,

Mr. Searlington. If you're not careful I might actually believe you love me."

He buried his hand in her mussed hair and yanked her mouth down to his. His mouth owning hers hard and fast, no questions. No need to ask for permission, she was his, and had afforded him this liberty long ago. "There is no question of whether I love you. I do, and if you don't know that, then I'm doing something wrong."

He saw the shy smile lift her lips, the one that always surfaced whenever he spoke about his love for her. She looked up at him with wide brown eyes that called to the very foundation of his core. "I know you love me... I'm just still so surprised that you do."

Two years and they always came back to this, Heart and her insecurity about their relationship. She was right; she didn't question whether Kenneth loved her, just questioned why he loved her. It was heartbreaking at times, frustrating at others. It bothered him most because it made him feel as if she didn't trust what they had, as if she always expected at some point in the future it would come to an end.

That shit wasn't an option. He was never letting her go. He just wished he didn't have to work so hard at convincing her of that fact.

"Stop," he ground out quickly. "Just stop. You know I hate it when you talk about yourself like this. I'm with you because I want to be."

Her brows knit together in question, but she paused and buried her face in his chest. She snuggled closer to him and he tightened his embrace in response. This was what they needed, more moments of falling into each other's arms, less time thinking about unreasonable insecurities that had no possibility of becoming reality. He'd fought through hell to make her his, there was no way he was ever going to let her go now that he knew what complete nirvana felt like. Heart Searlington was his now—as far as he was concerned—and always.

CHAPTER 3

$\mathscr{K}$enneth stood in his kitchen sipping a fresh cup of coffee. He drank it out of habit and not necessity. He was rested, no signs of the jetlag he should have been experiencing. He'd come home yesterday morning from a one-week Asian business trip. As much as he'd needed his bed, he couldn't begin to think about resting until he'd at least laid eyes on his wife.

Just the thought of that woman and the amazing way she made him feel had a smile tugging at his lips. His wife, his Heart, she made his mouth smile, his heart race, and his blood and body boil.

Between the near ten hours he'd slept when he arrived home and the subsequent eight he'd fallen into after making love to his wife, his body, soul, mind, and libido were all sharp, and ready for the day ahead.

He glanced down at his watch and realized he needed to head out the door quickly. He wasn't due into the office for another three hours, but he wanted to get a head start on catching up on his backlog of work he knew Abigail had waiting for him. After a week away from home, all Kenneth wanted was a little normalcy. A quiet meal with his wife, maybe kicking back on the couch to watch one of their countless

DVR'd backlist of TV shows. He needed to be connected to his anchor, get back to their regular routine.

He'd missed Heart, missed everything about being with her on a daily basis. The way she curled up inside of his arms when she slept, the way she bitched with him about not wiping down the sink counter when he washed his hands in the bathroom, the way she growled in monosyllabic tones until she'd infused her first dose of caffeine of the day.

He'd missed the way she'd pat her hand on her lap in invitation for him to rest his head there while they watched television. He'd missed the way she slowly stroked his long locks from scalp to tip until he was lulled into peaceful sleep. He'd missed the smooth sounds of her voice, the naturally sweet fragrance of her skin, damn; even the taste and feel of her had him longing for home.

She entered the kitchen and his smiled instantly widened. She was dressed in her formal captain's uniform, the white shirt and navy pants hugging the curves of her body in a delectable way. He smiled a little more, that material wasn't hugging her curves, it was outright strangling them and the sight of those hips, and that ass made his cock thicken up just a little and say good morning.

He reached for her, pulling her into his embrace and letting his hands travel down her back until they were filled with her round, firm globes. He smoothed his hands over them then gave them a long generous squeeze.

"Please remind me to thank whoever it is that makes these damn uniforms. I don't think there's a piece of lingerie made that makes my dick harder than the sight of you in this get up." He leaned down and placed an ample kiss on her full lips and reconsidered his plan to go into the office early. Work could wait, this shit right here needed his immediate attention.

He reached the button at the top of her uniform and felt her hands close around his. The motion made him lean up and break the kiss.

"What gives? I'm trying to show my wife how much I appreciate her."

Heart stepped back and away from him shaking her head. "Not

this morning," she said. "I've got a meeting at One Police Plaza today. You will not have me walking up in there looking like who did it and ran."

She knew him so well. He took extreme pride and pleasure in making certain she looked and felt thoroughly debauched every single time he got his hands on her. It had become his mission in life and he took it very seriously.

"I thought you had meetings yesterday?"

"I did, but that was something quick with the inspector. Today I've got to lay the facts of this new case we just caught out for a room full of bigwigs. I'll talk and they'll determine what I'm doing wrong and why the case hasn't been solved in the twenty-four hours since we picked it up."

She rolled her eyes and he could see her eyebrows pinching together in annoyance and frustration.

"Is this that case with the aide that worked in the governor's office?"

She nodded her head. "Yeah, we caught that, and now brass is all over me about it. So no, Mr. Searlington, no cookie for you this morning. I gotta step in a few. You want a ride, I can't take you all the way uptown, but at least I can drop you at the train to finish your commute to your office from lower Manhattan."

He nodded his head. "All right, go grab your stuff; I'll pour us two travel mugs of coffee."

She grabbed up her bag and keys and he held the door open for her while he balanced two travel mugs in one hand.

"Ladies first."

She stopped for a second, looking at him with a raised brow, and smiling eyes. "This has nothing to do with chivalry, does it?"

He laughed, "Baby, you know me so well. I just want to watch that ass in those pants for a little bit longer before I start my day."

She shook her head and rolled her eyes. "What am I going to do with you?" "Love me, baby...love me."

∾

*H*eart stood in her class-A Captain's dress uniform and formal jacket waiting to be called. God this uniform was making her itch. It was pretty much the same as her lieutenant's uniform, just a change in the insignia—one bar traded in for two and voila she had a captain's uniform. She hated this thing, always had. One of the greatest things about becoming a detective was getting rid of that damn uniform and burying it in the back of her closet. It only ever saw the light of day for formal situations within the department.

The fact that she was wearing it, coupled with that damn starched straight dress jacket, meant one thing—her attendance at a funeral. Either literally or figuratively, someone either had or was about to die and her professional appearance was being demanded as a result. She sat outside of the Bureau Chief's office tapping her tilted lid, wondering what the hell she had done to require her presence in front of the man that sat five steps and three stars up the rank ladder in the NYPD.

Fuck my life, she thought.

She knew exactly why she was here. These damn multiple murders on Ho Stroll. She didn't delude herself, she knew damn well the person, or persons sitting on the other side of that door didn't give a good goddamn about people ending up dead on Ho Stroll. She was being called to task for one reason alone, the governor's aide had ended up dead, brutally murdered, on a dank street in a Brooklyn slum, and this shit just couldn't be tolerated by NYPD brass.

The door creaked open signaling the start of what could only be a migraine in the making for her. These meetings were never fun and seeing that her captain's rank was the lowest rank in the room, she surmised this little meet and greet was about to turn into a 'let's fuck with the young captain in the room,' party.

Heart stood up at attention with her lid tucked neatly under her arm. "Bureau Chief Sheehan,

sir."

The middle-aged Caucasian man stood just a little under six feet tall with a solid build. His mostly salt and slightly pepper hair was cut into a very low regulation haircut, tapered at the sides, almost buzzed at the top. Green eyes fastened on to hers and acknowledged her display of respect to a senior officer.

"Captain Searlington, please enter." He stepped aside and ushered her into the large office. The first thing she noticed was a large conference table where four more men were seated. Three of them she recognized, the governor, the mayor, and the police commissioner.

There went her hope of getting out of this room with at least some of her hide intact. Those three faces were the three top administrative offices in New York. They were the leaders of the city and state, accompanied by the number one cop in their leading law enforcement agency. This was so not going to be a fun gathering for her. That shit was evidently clear by the matching puckered looks all three men were wearing, as if they were playing a game of pass the lemon. *These motherfuckers plan to have a Searlington feast today.*

Her stomach twisted a little either due to nervousness or maybe the coffee she drank this morning and was messing with her. Either way, she had the distinct desire to run for the nearest bucket and hurl. She discreetly reached into her pocket and slipped a couple of mints in her mouth. It was either that or embarrass herself in front of her bosses, and that shit was not even an option as far as Heart was concerned.

Sheehan directed her to the head of the table, while he took a seat next to the police commissioner. Heart acknowledged each of the other occupants before taking her seat. *All right*

Searlington, they may have come to feast, there's nothing you can do about that. Just do what Porter taught you to do, state the facts, keep it simple, own up to your mistakes, and offer a reasonable solution if allowed to. Anything else was out of her hands, and really didn't make sense to fret over.

It was the chief's office, but the governor was apparently leading this meeting because he was the first to speak.

"Captain, it's my understanding that you were the former commander of one of the premier investigative teams in the city. Your superiors speak very highly of your capabilities and your track record seems to support their confidence in you. Everyone has heard about the great

MacKenzie-Searlington and the way she's able to close the unclosable cases. I'm hoping that rings true for these Pitkin Avenue murders as well."

"Sir, I do have the best team. My detectives are working this case the way they work all cases, diligently, and efficiently."

"What leads do you have?" the commissioner asked.

"Sir, at the moment we're looking into the background of the victims to attempt to figure out why any of them would be targeted in such a manner."

"Do we have a serial killer on our hands in Brooklyn, Captain?" the mayor asked.

"Sir, that has yet to be determined. According to the medical examiner, all the young women were killed in the same manner. They were each sexually assaulted, bound, and strangled with professional grade fishing wire. Their bodies were also mutilated by a blade with serrated edges and the lacerations on their breasts were sewn up with surgical sutures. The M.E. believes that whoever the perpetrator is, he must have some medical training because the sutures were accurately placed.

"According to our preliminary investigation, the victims had very little in common. Two of the three women killed were prostitutes, but they didn't really hang out in the same crowds and don't seem to have anyone in common. At this time we can't seem to find a single reason why Ms. Silverson would have been connected with the first two victims. My detectives are out now searching Ms. Silverson's apartment and speaking with her family and friends to try to find out how she ended up in the perp's sights."

"Captain," Sheehan interjected. "I don't need to tell you that this matter is of pressing concern to us. Ms. Silverson was a valued member of the governor's team and we cannot have criminals feeling that they can get away with harming city and state officials."

Heart stilled every bone and muscle in her body to keep from opening her mouth or rolling her eyes. She knew this damn meeting had less to do with her providing a situation report for them; they just wanted to remind her that the only case that mattered was of the victim that had political connections.

Moments like these were where she truly missed having her predecessor Captain Porter around. He was well versed at playing in this political playground. He understood how to navigate the river of bullshit well enough to appease the higher ups and still protect his people and the citizens they were sworn to protect.

Heart wasn't built that way. Her natural reaction to this sort of favoritism was to call bullshit. Her shiny new captain's badge and bars dictated she bite down hard on the side of her tongue and let these fools talk...for now.

"This matter needs to be dealt with expediently," Sheehan continued. "Aside from the tactics you've mentioned here today, have you secured any other resources to help you pursue this case to a successful end?"

She nodded her head as she turned her gaze to the bureau chief. "Yes sir, we've also contacted the local FBI branch to get some help with dealing with this kind of situation."

The commissioner leaned forward. "Are you saying you're not equipped to take this case on,

Captain?"

Heart shook her head. *Keep it simple girl,* she said to herself. *Don't let them break you.* Her stomach threatened to turn, but she took a slow breath to ease the mild hint of nausea that was trying to grow in to something loud and ugly. *Man I've gotta stop drinking so much coffee. I hope to God I didn't let these fools stress me in to an ulcer.* She took a sip of water from the glass that sat directly in front of her, waiting for it to cleanse the foul taste that was filling her mouth; despite the mouth full of mints she had hiding in her cheeks.

"Commissioner Greer, I have every confidence in my detectives; they are the best at what they do and I think they're more than capable. But I've trained my detectives to recognize that being the best at something doesn't mean you know everything, it just means you use the resources available to you better than most. That means calling in help when you need it. The FBI has much more experience with this kind of crime and considering how pressing this issue is, I think we need to use everything in our arsenal in order to close this case.

Heart watched the room, taking in body language, gauging what the men in this room were thinking. They all had the outraged concern look going for them, shoulders hunched up, elbows leaning forward on the table, faces pulled tight, brow line furrowed. Every single one of them including the strange man no one had bothered to introduce wore that angry seriousness on their faces, all except the governor.

There was anger there; he seemed agitated and tired, like he was worrying about something. Gone was the polished veneer that graced the television screen every time he held a news conference. Now, he looked almost sick, pale skin tinged with a strange green hue. Eyes spiked with lines of red. The knot of his tie was loose and his suit looked just this side of rumpled. Acceptable for the average everyday Joe? Yes. But not for a sitting governor, for a man of his stature it was a problem.

What's that about, she wondered.

"I'm glad you agree, Captain," the governor offered. "Because we're going to send you help." The governor turned his attention to the strange man that sat there quietly through the duration of her inquisition.

"Captain Searlington, please meet Supervisory Special Agent, Caleb Weaver. He is going to be sent to your precinct to help your team find this killer."

Heart looked over to Agent Weaver. He was African-American with chocolate brown skin just a shade darker than hers. His head was bald and his face was free of facial hair. What she could see of his sitting form revealed a fit physique. She couldn't really tell how tall he was in his current seated position because he was leaning slightly to one side in his chair. But looking into hazel brown eyes, she saw an awareness that she always looked for when bringing someone into her command. This man had it in spades. As far as she was concerned, if he had half as much skill as that cocky ass crooked smile suggested he did, he might be useful to Heart. Superagent man coupled with her investigators, and this perpetrator's days on the street just might be numbered.

"She was my family," the governor said with a deluge of ragged desperation dripping from his voice.

Heart's cop brain took notice of that desperation. For some reason it struck her as odd. She didn't quite understand why, at least not yet, but she filed that away for later examination.

The governor paused, looked down into the glass of water he'd pulled in front of him and cleared his throat of the thick emotion that seemed to be clawing at his words. "She was an integral part of my executive family and I want the son of a bitch that did this dead, or behind bars. I've added an extra line item to the mayor's budget to help offset the cost of manpower that I expect to be used toward closing this case. Whatever resources you require, Captain, I will make certain you have them."

The governor rose from his seat quickly and everyone else seated at the table followed suit. All of his lesser ranking officials stumbling over themselves to show respect to the governor. He left before most of them could make it halfway out of their seat. The mayor and police commissioner followed immediately. Heart was left alone with her bureau chief and the F.B.I. agent.

"Captain, I'm sure you understand how pressing this matter is. Don't make us look bad," Sheehan said. "Dismissed."

She nodded her head and stepped toward the door with a sure stride. When she reached the door she looked over her shoulder at the agent still in the room and asked, "Are you coming, Agent Weaver?"

CHAPTER 4

*H*eart moved through her precinct quickly pushing toward her office with SSA Weaver following closely behind. "Smyth," she yelled without stopping or looking to see if Smyth were anywhere in the vicinity. It didn't matter if he was near or not, someone would get the message to him that he was being summoned by his captain.

She unbuttoned her formal jacket, gladly hanging it on the back of her chair. Before she was fully seated behind her desk she had that miserable clip-on tie removed and the top button on her shirt collar opened. When she finally felt the comforting cushions of her desk chair touch the backs of her legs, she pulled a long and loud breath into her lungs.

"Have a seat, Agent Weaver."

He took a seat in front of her desk and stretched out the long legs that had been hidden under the conference table when they'd first met. Shortly after he sat she heard a quiet tap on her door, and her second stepped inside of the room.

"'Sup, Cap?" Bryan said as he walked toward her desk.

"Lieutenant Bryan Smyth, this is Supervisory Special Agent Caleb Weaver. The governor has assigned him to our task force to find the perp in this Ho Stroll case." She turned quickly to Weaver. "Weaver, this is my second in command, Lieutenant Bryan Smyth." She watched the two men shake hands and pass cordial professional acknowledgement between the two of them.

"Smyth, I need a sit-rep on the case. We need to bring Weaver up to speed, and then the team needs to meet him so he can tell us what he's adding to the party."

She handed Weaver the case file on her desk and turned her attention toward her lieutenant.

"What the hell was Silverson doing on Ho Stroll, Smyth?"

Bryan took a slow breath and eased himself forward to meet Heart's gaze. "We don't know. We canvassed her work, and her home, and no one can come up with a reasonable idea as to why she would be in East New York at all."

He opened the notepad he'd pulled from his back pocket and began flipping through the pages. "According to her colleagues, everyone loved her. She cared for the sick and downtrodden and if you can believe the praise, she probably walked on water too. Everyone we spoke to said she should be nominated for sainthood."

Heart rolled her eyes. People were a trip, they cursed you in life, but the minute you closed your eyes to this world, they would scream how perfect you were from the rooftops. "If everyone's singing the same song it was either true, or more likely rehearsed. You think this is the line people were told to recite?"

Smyth shrugged his shoulders. "Hard to tell, Cap. These are politicians we're talking about. They're lying even when they're telling the truth."

Heart scratched her head in frustration. She could already see this case was going to be a pain in the ass. This was the very reason she hated high-profile cases. People wanted them solved, but they lied and schemed to keep their secrets hidden, making it harder for her cops to do their jobs.

"Was she working on anything that could have gotten her killed?" she asked.

"We asked, we were told that whatever projects she was working on were highly classified and we don't have high enough security clearance to look at them."

Heart turned to Agent Weaver. "Is there anything you can do about this, or do I have to get the district attorney and the federal prosecutor involved. Just in case you don't know, I really hate dealing with lawyers, so if there's a way around this bullshit without involving them, I'm all

for it."

Agent Weaver shrugged his shoulders. "I can make a few calls and see what I can do, but don't hold your breath. These politicians can be a real piece of work when they want to be." She rolled her eyes and moved on. "Family?" she asked Bryan.

Bryan shook his head. "None to speak of. She was orphaned as a teenager and raised by her mother's brother. The uncle died a few years back, leaving Silverson alone. We did track down her roommate. Tonia Daniels is also an aide for the governor. The two have shared an apartment in Bed-Stuy since their junior year in college."

Heart slammed her hands down on the desk. "Dammit, Smyth, I need more than that. That girl crossed paths with a killer in our backyard for a reason. Your team better figure out why. Call the team into the conference room so we can all hear what Weaver has to add to the mix."

Bryan's departure ended with the click of her door. She turned to the agent on loan to her with determined eyes. "You'd better have something useful to add to this mess, Weaver.

Otherwise I'll ship you right back down to Quantico."

Weaver nodded and Heart stood up, led them out of her office, and into the conference room. Bryan's team sat waiting. They watched Weaver carefully as he stood on the other side of Heart.

"So Cap," Santini said. "We're bringing the feds in already? We've only been at this for a couple of days."

Heart pinched the bridge of her nose, something she found herself doing more frequently since she became captain. At this rate, she was going to cause some sort of damage if she didn't find a new way to deal with work-related annoyances like smart-assed detectives.

"Santini, you're right, we have only been at this a couple of days. But today I was called into an impromptu meeting with the governor, mayor, bureau chief, and the top cop. They've assigned us Agent Weaver," she announced. She gave Weaver a nod, giving him the floor.

"I've been assigned to assist in solving these crimes. I've been tracking a killer who has a similar M.O.," he offered.

She introduced Bryan's five detectives to Weaver and waited as they each shared their investigative findings—findings that didn't really add up to much.

She watched as her second stood up and walked to the dry erase board and pointed at the three post-mortem photos of the victims. "We need more than this," Bryan said. "We can't do shit with the little we've found so far. Are there any connections between these three women?"

Grazzo shook his head. "Other than their manner of death...no."

"Agent Weaver," Heart said. "What can you tell us about the killer you've been tracking?"

Weaver opened up his briefcase and removed three large jacket folders. "Seattle,

Washington, Imperial Beach, California, and Miami, Florida," he said as he busied himself removing individual file folders from the jackets and spreading them across the table.

"In each of these cities the same killer has killed four women. They were all young and attractive, and all were prostitutes. They were each bound by the arms and ankles and strangled with fishing wire. He mutilated each of them by performing rudimentary mastectomies postmortem. He also raped them post-mortem and carved the numeral seven into their labia. After the perpetrator was done, he would pose their arms crosswise against their chests. He's hit cities at the edge of the continental U.S., so the press is dubbing him the four corners killer." "God this bastard is sick," Ramirez said from the other side of the table.

Heart watched as the seasoned detective rubbed her hands up and down her arms. Heart understood Ramirez' movements, she herself felt a cold chill zipping down her backbone that made her want to rub warmth back into her own skin. The more details the agent in the room revealed about the previous murders, the colder Heart felt.

"Are you certain this freak has moved into Brooklyn?" Heart asked. "I mean, we're northeast, but there are states further north than New York on the Eastern seaboard." Her need to protect her city raged inside of her. The part of Brooklyn she was sworn to protect had enough problems with poverty and crime, they didn't need to add a deranged killer to the mix for entertainment.

"I don't know yet," Weaver said. "It looks like him, but until the medical examiner's report comes through, I won't know for certain."

Bryan returned to the conference table, looking through the files Agent Weaver had placed there. "What do the feds know about this killer, Weaver?"

"We're looking for a twenty-five to thirty-five year old white male. He's someone with formal medical training, but probably not a doctor as evidenced by the quality of surgical wounds and sutures placed in the victims. He's a psychopath, a sexual sadist. He gets off on the torture of others, but can't perform sexually until the women are completely at his mercy, that's why he rapes them after he kills them.

"As with most psychopaths, he's very intelligent, charming, he's able to mimic empathy and emotion so well people often have no idea how sick these people are. If you look in his past you'll probably find some instances of animal torture as well as aggressive behavior in the family.

"Most psychopaths are able to hold down good jobs, they're often very intelligent and have a college-level education. We're thinking he's probably a transient worker of sorts. With his medical knowledge maybe someone in the military that worked in a medical capacity or even some sort of traveling nurse. Either way, his job allows him to travel, giving him opportunities to kill in these cities."

Heart watched as her second and his team took notes. They might not like the fact that the FBI was involved in their case, but they were more concerned with finding this killer than cushioning their pride.

"So why is he attacking local prostitutes?" Bryan asked. "Does he have a beef with them, does he hate all women, was his mother a prostitute?"

Weaver shook his head. "Most psychopaths grow up in a completely normal nuclear family. We think he's preying on prostitutes simply because they are accessible and their community is the least likely to report a predator amongst them."

Heart nodded her head. "All right then. For now, I want to focus on the victims. Smyth, break your team up, and have them find us some more information on the victims' lives. After you're done, you, Weaver, and I are going to devise a plan of attack to get through the bullshit with His Excellency and his staff."

Bryan's shoulders shook with laughter. "His Excellency?"

"Yeah, that's the honorific title used for the governor."

"They teach you that in Captain's school?" Bryan asked.

She could always trust her second to lighten the mood when a case was about to make her spaz out.

"As a matter of fact, yeah, they did. I've also been forced to hang in circles with some of the loftier folk in the city over the last couple of years, so you know...I pick up stuff."

Her detectives laughed, used to the levity passed between their captain and lieutenant. Weaver on the other hand looked like he was uncertain what his reaction should be to all of their laughter.

"It's all right, Agent Weaver," Heart said as she relaxed her stance a little, giving the agent leave to do the same. "We've learned very early on that laughter keeps us sane when we're working on something this intense."

The silent man nodded his head, while a small smile lifted full caramel lips. Heart turned back to her detectives and pointed to the photo of their three dead victims on the board.

"We've got to figure this thing out, guys, before there's a fourth victim." The laughter bled out of her voice and was replaced by a deliberate and thoughtful tone. "We don't know why any of these women were killed yet, but my guess is that Silverson is the key to unlocking all of the rest. The executive branch may not want us poking around in their business, but that's exactly what we're going to do. Someone had to know something about why this uptown girl was found in a downtown gutter and I'd bet my last bullet it's someone who works in the governor's office."

CHAPTER 5

$\mathcal{K}$enneth slowly tilted his head to stretch the achy muscles of his neck. He looked down in the lower right corner of his computer screen and noted the time. Six hours he'd sat in this same spot behind his desk and plowed through endless contracts, settlements, and proposals that would continue to secure his company's success and growth.

He thought about continuing his forward motion through the pile of things that needed his attention on his desk, but just as he was about to grab yet another file, he hesitated. He snatched his hand back as if the files were covered in flames and he pressed his back into the comfortable cushions of his chair.

Kenneth took a slow breath in reflecting on the differences he'd noticed about himself since he married Heart. Before their marriage, he'd thought nothing of spending the night working at this very desk, formulating plans to beat his competitors. Now, he was still concerned with beating the competition, but if he couldn't do it before six in the evening, it would have to wait until he returned in the morning, because his wife was waiting for him.

His dual need to keep his business successful while spending quality time with his wife, forced him to make some hard decisions.

The first was he absolutely couldn't do this alone anymore. He'd needed help to balance it all.

Once the decision was made to find someone to help him carry the load at the office, he knew exactly who he had in mind for the vice president position. Elliot Alan Quillen, III was his fraternity brother from his college days and had remained one of his closest friends since.

Alan hadn't officially agreed to take on the position of vice president when Kenneth made his offer. Instead he'd agreed to help Kenneth for as long as Kenneth needed him to with the added caveat that Kenneth would at least make a good faith effort to find someone to permanently fill the position at a later time. Alan had been in serious need of a change of scenery, accepting Kenneth's offer and moving from his home in Los Angeles across the country to settle in New York just to help his friend.

He laughed at himself. Alan had taken to his office like he'd been born in it. The man had never worked in commercial real estate, but he had a unique business skill set from spending years running his grandfather's billion-dollar company that translated well into qualities Kenneth needed in a second in command.

Kenneth shook his head; he was still amazed at how different his life was. Not long ago he'd sat in this very office offended that the then Lieutenant MacKenzie had scoffed his advances and essentially ignored him. The rejection he could deal with, it was the ignoring him part that drove him crazy and eventually drove him right into her arms.

And now, two years later, all he wanted to do was remain in those arms. The rush of love and life that surrounded him while he rested in those arms kept him eager to return to them every minute of every day. He'd even resorted to arranging his work life to allow him to spend as much time in her presence as possible.

He began shutting down his computer when he heard a tap on his door.

"Ken, you got a minute?" Alan asked as he walked into the room.

"Sure."

"I've narrowed down the best of three prospectus campaigns that I think will work for the Primus account we're trying to land. I just need you to sign off on which one you want and to secure a date for the meeting with Ian Shaw for the presentation."

Kenneth rolled his eyes at the mention of Ian Shaw's name. Ian was a spoiled daddy's boy who didn't know his ass from his elbow when it came to hard work and creativity. He was a trust fund kid who was playing with daddy's money while he decided how he was going to make his mark on the world.

He wasn't exactly his favorite potential client, but the man's company had very deep pockets making him one of the few people capable of purchasing the very expensive set of office buildings Kenneth and Alan were attempting to sell.

It wasn't that Shaw had ever really done anything in particular to make Kenneth dislike him. It was just a difference of opinion on where their values fell. Kenneth enjoyed being wealthy, but he never let his bottom line define who he was or how he viewed or treated people. With Shaw, if you didn't have as much money as he did, you pretty much didn't exist to him.

Kenneth despised that kind of snobbery, but the truth was there were several of his clients that sought his services out for the sheer fact that he was just as wealthy and connected as they were. Kenneth dealt in high-end properties. They were places that were coveted by heavy rollers who needed to show their status by owning the most expensive everything, including business spaces and residences.

He might not have liked socializing with people like Shaw, but he damn sure wouldn't turn down the entitled little prick's money anytime soon.

"Do I really need to be there? I mean, you've got this, Alan."

Alan laughed. "Yeah, I do have this. But Shaw wants you there. I think he wants to get a selfie of you and him signing the contracts so he can post it to his social media and brag about his purchase to his many followers."

Alan was joking, but Kenneth cringed at the possible truth that rested in his statement.

"Come on, Ken, you know buying a building from you is a status symbol to a man like

Shaw. The fantasy just isn't the same if he doesn't get to be schmoozed by the great man himself. Not to mention, I've about had my fill of him, so I'm instituting the bro code on this one."

Kenneth shrugged his shoulders. "I'm failing to see how 'bros before ho's applies here."

Alan shook his head. "Not that code, the other code. No leaving your frat brother alone in the company of a pompous asshole for more than fifteen minutes at a time."

"I'd almost forgotten that one," he responded. "Any weekday is fine, just give the date and time to Abby and she'll put it on my calendar." Kenneth reached for the files in Alan's hand and read through them quickly before selecting which plan he wanted Alan to implement for the sales pitch.

He waved a hand in response to the, "Later boss," Alan threw over his shoulders on his way out of Kenneth's office. He went back to his end of day ritual of locking away files, securing his computer and clearing his desk of the day's workload. Just as he was preparing to lift himself out of his seat his cell rang.

His face relaxed into a happy smile when he saw the familiar number. He swiped his finger across the screen and laughed into the phone.

"What's the matter, Grant, your woman can't keep you busy enough so you're calling me at midnight France time?"

"Hi, Uncle Kenneth."

The smile dropped from his face as the angelic image of his sweet seven-year-old niece danced across his eyes. *Shit, Searlington, way to ruin the only child of your dead twin sister.*

"Hey, Merri, what are you doing up this time of night. Is something going on, sweetheart? Is your daddy okay?"

He waited anxiously for the answer. If something had happened it would take him too long to get to her. He sat up in his chair straighter, his muscles poised for action and braced for bad news. Whatever it was he would handle it, he would make it right for this child. He'd promised his sister he would always make certain she was taken care of and Kenneth never went back on his promises.

"Daddy's fine," she said. "I just missed you, and I couldn't sleep so I called you."

His body instantly relaxed and he let out the breath he'd been holding. "I miss you too, little one."

"I'm not little anymore, Uncle Kenneth, I'm seven now."

Kenneth laughed, she was right she was getting bigger. The last set of pictures Andrew had sent him showed her looking more and more like her mother Karolyn every day. Whenever he thought about how much Merri resembled him and his late twin sister it always filled his heart with an equal mixture of pride and pain.

Karolyn had been taken from him before either of them had been able to heal the rift that had existed for years between them. It wasn't until his sister was dying in his arms that he'd realized how much his absence had compromised his sister's ability to thrive.

And now he was left with his beautiful niece, and he knew he would never squander the time he had with her. He traveled to Paris frequently, and whenever Merridith had a break from school, her father William would allow her to vacation with him and his wife.

"I'm sorry, you're right," his smiled broadened. "You are a big girl now, almost grown up now that you're seven. So what can I do for you, young lady?"

"Daddy says he's going to be very busy this summer because he's starting a special line. I thought maybe I could come stay with you and Aunt Heart while Daddy works."

Kenneth thought about it. French schools ended their term at the very end of June or the beginning of July and didn't resume until the first week in September. That would be eight weeks. Kenneth and Heart had kept the young girl for a week or two at a time, but never as long as she was requesting now. He flipped through his calendar and realized he didn't have anything pending during that time.

"I will have to check with your dad and Heart to see if they're both all right with it, but I would love to have you spend some time with us."

He heard a loud and happy scream come through the phone and he pulled it away to spare his hearing.

"Merri, your dad is sleeping, don't wake him up."

"Sorry, Uncle Kenneth. I can't wait to see you and Aunt Heart. Give her a kiss for me."

"I will do, now go to bed, sprite."

He sat staring at the phone for a while after Merridith hung up. Warmth filled him and a smile he couldn't control lifted his features. He loved that little girl something fierce. It almost bordered on pain. There was nothing he wouldn't do to keep her happy and safe. She'd suffered unimaginable loss in her young years, and he would make certain she saw more happiness than sadness for the rest of his days if he could.

He pulled Merridith's picture up on his phone and smiled again. She was so beautiful, a miniature version of his sister, the same soft angles and curves on her face, the same bright crystal blue eyes, and the same long midnight locks of hair. Merridith shared so many of the same features he'd shared with his sister that she could be mistaken for his child. *I wonder if our kids will look so much like Karolyn and me.*

He stopped in mid reach as realization washed over him. *Our kids? Exactly which kids would those be? Could they be the imaginary ones that you and your wife haven't spoken word one about having?*

He sat back for a minute, taking time to let the musings of his mind marinate. Yeah, he and Heart had never spoken about having children. He'd proposed to her and married her all in the span of a couple of weeks; there'd been no time to have those kinds of conversations before they'd wed. But it had been two years, and still, the topic of children had never come up.

Heart had taken it upon herself to go on the pill when she'd been promoted. He'd understood. She was taking on a great deal of responsibility in an organization where often an

"all boys club" mentality applied. Being out on maternity leave a few months after you've been promoted captain wouldn't have been a wise career move at that time. *Yeah that was then, but what about now?*

Two years had passed, she was settled in her job, and they were settled in their marriage. Maybe now might be a good time to at least broach the subject. And exactly what did he plan on saying when he in fact raised the subject?

I want kids?

Did he? He liked kids, he loved his niece Merridith, but he wasn't really sure he was ready to be a father to his own children.

Honestly, with as many times as Heart had forgotten to take the damn pills he was surprised they hadn't conceived already.

But just because you could have conceived, does that really mean you want to conceive?

He couldn't answer that, not with any reasonable amount of certainty. He knew he loved his wife, he knew he loved making love to his wife. He needed inside her at least once a day. The only time he gave her reprieve was during her cycle. And to tell the truth, that was more because of her than him. She refused, it didn't much matter to him, but it was a taboo subject as far as his wife was concerned. But trust, he knew the exact moment she was off the rag and the minute she was, he was taking his rightful place again seated to the hilt inside of her tight, wet, warmth.

Damn, just the thought of being inside her again made his dick throb and twitch. He reached down and adjusted himself.

Settle down boy, we weren't supposed to be thinking about sexing Heart. We're thinking about fatherhood. Am I really ready to be a father?

Honestly, he couldn't really answer that question with absolute certainty, but he knew one thing, he wasn't exactly turned off by the idea either. Apparently he and his wife needed to have a conversation sooner rather than later.

∾

*H*eart slowly rubbed the aching throb in her left temple. The dull pain was going to drive her mad. She slowly opened her eyes to glance at the two men sitting across her desk from her. One was her second in command, the other a decorated federal agent. Between the three of them sitting in her office, there were decades of investigative experience and yet none of them were making any leeway in this case.

"Someone please tell me why none of us are able find out anything about this girl's work life beyond the song and dance her job is providing us?" Heart groaned with frustration.

"The girl didn't have a regular job, Cap," Bryan answered.

"Smyth is right," Weaver interjected. "This girl worked for the highest authority in this state.

If the governor's office doesn't want us sniffing around, then we're probably not going to find anything."

"Honestly, I've been trying to be nice because I really don't want the headache of trying to get a warrant to search her work materials at the governor's office. Judges can be kind of iffy when you're asking them to piss off the higher ups on the political food chain."

She resumed rubbing her temple to displace some of the tension that was bundled up in that one area on the side of her head. "Any other suggestions?" she asked the two men seated across from her.

"I have one, but I know you're not going to like it," Smyth said.

"At this point, I doubt there's anything about this case that I'm going to like. What is it,

Smyth?"

"Porter and Big Willie."

Heart instantly started shaking her head.

"Hell no."

Weaver looked between the two of them, trying to follow the internal conversation she and Smyth were having.

"You need them," Bryan said.

"Like I need a bullet in the head," she countered.

"Who the hell are Porter and Big Willie?" Weaver asked.

Bryan answered. "The former captain and lieutenant of this precinct."

"Two overbearing pains in the ass that I would prefer to keep out of this," she said.

"You don't think they can help?" Weaver asked.

"No, I'm pretty sure they can, there's not much about police work those two can't figure out," Heart answered.

"Then what's the problem?" Weaver continued.

"Porter and Big Willie are an experience I'd rather not have at the moment."

Bryan laughed. "Looks like you don't have much of a choice."

"Smyth, if I've got to deal with those two, I'm gonna need a drink. Set it up so they'll meet us at the diner. I'm going to see if they can give us a corner in the back room so we can get some work done without too many eyes watching us."

Bryan and Weaver left Heart alone in her office. She reached for the telephone and called the diner to secure a semi-private spot for them to meet. When she was done she picked up her cell phone and softly touched a familiar thumbnail photo.

"Hello, Mrs. Searlington," the warmth that surrounded the greeting made the flesh on her arms raise in tiny goose bumps. Two years married to the man and just the sound of his voice calling her name was enough to excite her.

"Hello, Mr. Searlington. How are you?"

"I'm okay, but I'd be better if I had my wife in my arms right now."

The smile on her face stretched even wider. Kenneth certainly knew how to make a woman feel needed.

"I'm a little annoyed. Hard case is kicking my ass right now. Bryan and I are actually going over to the diner on Linden to meet up with Porter and Big Willie." "In need of some old-school guidance?" he asked.

"Pretty much," she answered. "I'm a great street worker, but learning to navigate the pitfalls of diplomacy isn't really in my forte. The two O.G.'s spent the better part of their administrative careers doing it. I need whatever help they can give me on getting politicians to open up."

"How are you getting home? I have your car."

She nodded her head. The plan when they'd left this morning was for her to drop him off while she continued on to her meeting with the higher-ups. But the truth was her husband had taken one look at her worried expression and taken the keys out of her hand. They'd agreed that he would pick her up, or she'd catch a car service home.

"I know, I'm sure one of the guys will give me a ride if I ask, I know you're tired, you can just head straight home."

"Never too tired to come get my wife," his smooth voice sailed through the phone making the fine hairs on her arms stand up.

"All right," she said.

"I've got a few things here that need my attention. I was going to leave them for tomorrow, but since I'm meeting up with you, I'll finish what I need to do here then head out to get you."

"Great," she said. "See you then."

As she ended the call she heard a tap on her door. She waved Agent Weaver in and began collecting her belongings.

"Ready, Captain?"

She nodded. "Is Smyth in the squad room?"

"No," Weaver said. "He already left, said he was going to pick up your former bosses, said they're close by. I told Smyth I'd give you a ride there."

"All right then, Agent, let's roll."

CHAPTER 6

"So, why don't you want to bring your former captain and lieutenant in on this case?"

Heart pulled her attention from the car window and glanced at Weaver. She gave the question consideration. The truth was, Porter and Big Willie were two of the best cops she'd ever known. She'd learned so much working under both of them. If she was half the investigator everyone claimed she was it was only because those two had taught her how to be.

But for some reason, having them guide her on this case made her uneasy. Porter had left his beloved seventy-fourth precinct in her care, he'd trusted her to take care of it, and keep it thriving and growing. Going to him now on a case like this just made her feel like maybe he hadn't made the correct decision in choosing a successor.

"I don't have a problem with consulting them," she said. She folded her arms across her chest and turned her gaze back to the streets passing in the window. She heard a small chuckle pass Agent Weaver's lips.

"You do know I'm a profiler right? I get paid to figure people out for a living."

It seemed Weaver's bullshit meter worked just as well as hers.

She wasn't really interested in hearing what his observations were at the moment. Fortunately they were nearing the dinner so being stuck in the car with him and his profiler skills would soon come to an end.

"Just pull into this parking lot on the right and we're here."

They walked into the diner and were greeted by the practiced smile of a petite Latina woman.

"Captain MacKenzie," the woman beamed. "It's good to see you again, follow me, you're friends are in the back."

"MacKenzie?" she heard Weaver ask from behind her.

"Long story," she uttered. Not feeling inclined to answer his question; she followed the woman to the back where Bryan, her former captain and lieutenant were seated at a dark corner in the back room of the diner.

Big Willie was the first to spot her as she neared the table. "Baby Girl, how you doing?" he asked with a warm smile. He lifted a meaty hand out to her and she shook it, giving him a warm smile in return. She turned to David Porter, her former captain and godfather to her husband. Porter was responsible for refining her skills as an investigator. He also happened to be the closest thing Heart had to a father-in-law. The man had molded and shaped her husband in to the amazing man she loved today, a fact she would spend the rest of her days being grateful for.

She shook his hand and then hooked a thumb over her shoulder at Agent Weaver. "Porter,

Big Willie, this is Agent Caleb Weaver of the FBI."

The agent smiled and offered his hand to the man closest to him in greeting. "Big

Willie...huh?" Weaver asked with a raised brow and a glib tone.

Heart rolled her eyes; she knew what was coming next. Big Willie clasped Weaver's hand in his paw-like hand and gave it a not-so-gentle squeeze. Willie was and always would be that guy that put motherfuckers in their place and let you know from jump he was not to be fucked with. As long as you respected that, you and he would have no problems. By the looks of the "fuck with me if you want to" expression written across Willie's features, Agent Weaver was about to find that out the hard way.

"Yeah," Willie's rough, low-timbered voice filled the air. "Or Lieutenant Seyah, if that makes you feel better."

She saw Agent Weaver's Adams apple bounce just a little as he swallowed. *Message received loud and clear.*

"Yes sir, Big Willie's fine with me," Agent Weaver said with an almost yelp-like quality to his voice. He turned his attention quickly to Porter and greeted him with a handshake as well. He nodded to Bryan, and moved to hold out a chair for Heart to sit down in.

She hesitated for a moment; chivalry wasn't something to be expected in her line of work.

You were either one of the boys or you weren't, there was no time to get caught up in such niceties. She finally nodded out a thank you and sat down at the large round table.

"So," Big Willie began. "What the hell do you want with us, Searlington?"

Heart just shook her head. That was Big Willie getting straight to the point, cutting through the shit.

"I'm sure you two already know we're working the hooker murders that took place on Ho

Stroll."

The two men nodded and she continued. "Well only two of the vics can be confirmed as hookers. The third young woman was actually an aide in the governor's office."

Out of the corner of her eye she saw the waitress laden down with serving trays enter the emptied dining room. She stopped talking long enough for the waitress to place their usual faire of Buffalo wings, tortilla chips and salsa, and the all-important never-ending beer pitcher. That was the beauty of having these sorts of meetings in a regular spot. They didn't even have to order; most times their order was pretty much waiting for them the moment they came in.

When the waitress was gone and closed the door to the private area, Heart took a hearty sip of the cold, golden, frothy beverage sitting in front of her.

"We're catching hell trying to collect info about this aide, Silverson," Heart said.

"Anything turn up in the original canvass?" Porter asked.

Heart shook her head. "Nothing more than the, 'she was great and should be named a saint,' song." She put her glass of beer down and filled her dish with wings and chips. She looked across the table at her lieutenant. "Smyth, did your team find anything out the second time around?"

Her second nodded. "Yeah, Cap. After we broke this morning, I had them go to Silverson's coworkers' homes. I figured they might be a little more open if they weren't in the office with all eyes on them. Ramirez said the vic's roommate said the girl was pretty much struggling financially a few years back. Said Silverson had to work two dinky jobs just to be able to afford part-time status at a local city college. Then a few years ago, Silverson appears to come into some money. Starts doubling up on classes, manages to graduate early, and finishes grad school the same way."

Heart nodded; at least this was more than they'd had in the last couple of day. "Did the roommate say how Silverson came into the money?"

"She believed it came from some sort of scholarship the vic told her she'd been awarded." Bryan dipped his wing in some of the ranch dressing on his plate and took a bite before continuing. "I had Grazzo and Jenson check out the Financial Aid and Bursar's office of her school. According to the school, she didn't have any sort of scholarship on file."

"Let me guess," Heart added. "Tuition bills were paid in cash?"

Bryan shook his head. "Nope, the school switched over to an all-electronic system two years before the vic started attending the school. The school no longer accepts cash or personal checks in person. You have to pay through credit, debit, or electronic wire transfer."

Heart smiled. "Please tell me we've tracked down her wealthy source," Heart pointed her fork at Bryan while she spoke.

"Not yet, but the tech guys at the department are working on it.

They said they should have something first thing in the morning. The roommate hinted that she thought the money was coming from a rich boyfriend. She said she never met the guy, if he in fact existed, but she just got the feeling that Silverson was seeing someone that didn't want to be noticed."

"Well it seems like you two are running good police work, so again I ask why the hell are we here?" Big Willie asked.

"'Cause I'm about to lose my fucking mind trying to get someone in this girl's office to talk to our people," Heart answered.

Porter laughed and took a large swallow of his beer. "Politicians giving you hell, Captain

Searlington?"

Heart's eyes glinted into narrow slits. Was it in poor taste to tell your former boss and quasi father-in-law to fuck off?

"Porter, you know I don't deal well in bullshit, and that's all these folks seem to be dishing. I was pulled into a meeting with brass. The governor and mayor were in attendance, along with the top cop and bureau chief. The governor assigned Agent Weaver to us and basically told me that however large the check was for manpower, he would sign it, just get the job done." Porter and Willie stopped in mid-chew to look at her and then each other.

"She must have been an important aide for the state to be willing to dish out that kind of cash to the mayor and the department. What exactly did Ms. Silverson do at the governor's office?" Porter asked.

"That's just it, Porter," Heart said. "I don't know. Every time we try to get an answer to that question we're met with silence and bullshit about not being able to disclose government information to those of us without the proper security clearance."

"What did the governor have to say about Silverson?" Willie asked.

"The last time I saw or spoke to the governor was at this sit-rep meeting with brass earlier today. He was very intense about us closing this case. It's very obvious he wants an arrest and conviction on this quickly."

"What do you mean by that, Searlington?" Willie asked.

There weren't many that could read her, but three of the four men sitting at this table with her had spent years studying her. She didn't have to say that something was bothering her about the case for them to know it.

"Willie, I can't put my finger on it, but there was something just off about the governor's reaction to all of this. I mean yeah, Silverson was his aide and all, but he acted like this was personal, not like a boss who'd lost an employee, but something more."

Willie nodded toward Weaver. "What about you super-agent man? What do you say about the governor's reaction to all of this."

Weaver wiped his mouth with a napkin and reached for his glass of beer. "He was intense.

Last night my superiors pulled me from a case I've been working for months and told me to report to downtown for a meet about this case. I'm assuming it was on the governor's say so. I'm not exactly certain why, but he definitely is very passionate about finding whoever is responsible for Ms. Silverson's death."

Willie scratched at his chin probably more out of habit than the fact that it actually itched.

He held Agent Weaver's gaze.

"So why did the governor call in the feds so early, Agent? I mean, PD is just getting started.

The feds are kind of a last ditch effort."

Weaver nodded. "True, but some of the major details of this case match several murders that took place around the country."

"Same perp?" Willie asked. Weaver nodded.

"The governor thinks this is the work of a serial killer, doesn't he?" Big Willie questioned.

"Possibly, we won't know until we get more info from the medical examiner," Weaver answered.

Porter placed his forearms on the table on either side of his plate and gave Heart and thoughtful look. "I don't know which possibility is worse, the fact that we might have a serial killer on the streets of East

New York or the fact that you're thinking the governor might somehow be involved in this girl's death."

He took a sip from his glass of beer and locked gazes with Heart. "That is what you're thinking right?"

"Porter, I don't..."

He held up a hand halting her.

"Cut the bullshit. Please tell me you're not trying to pin this shit on the governor of the state of New York, MacKenzie."

Heart rolled her eyes. Porter's use of her maiden name was a clear indication that he was deadly serious. He'd only called her MacKenzie when shit was about to blow up and he was trying to get to the bottom of it.

"Porter, I don't know that I suspect the governor of anything. My gut's telling me I need to talk to the man. I don't know why yet."

Porter sucked his teeth and then leaned back in his seat. "Between me and Willie we might be able to pull enough favors together to get you a sit down with the governor. But MacKenzie, there are going to be some ground rules if we agree to do this. First off, you'd better have a clearer understanding of what you want to ask. Don't go in there accusing the man without some very solid probable cause. Next, you're going to meet him some place other than his office. If you go up there, he'll shut up and stand behind all of his political bullshit to keep from answering your questions. Finally, you are a newly appointed captain in the NYPD. Just because you've been their golden child up until now, doesn't mean they won't crucify you if you poke the wrong bear. This is the governor, even for simple questioning, you'd better make sure your shit is tight. Got me?"

Heart nodded, she knew exactly what Porter was saying.

"Don't fuck up your career over this, baby girl," Willie added. "Work smart."

She looked across the table to Bryan and they both gave a synchronous nod. This shit was not going to be fun...she needed another beer.

∼

Kenneth walked into the door of the diner and gave a cursory look around for familiar faces.

*H*e caught sight of Bryan sitting at the bar with a man Kenneth didn't recognize. The man was black, fit, and tall, with a dark complexion and a bald—purposely so if his matching cleanshaven face was any indication. Stiff shoulders, imposing and animated movements of his arms, loud voice, yeah, this guy had cocky law enforcement personnel written all over him.

Kenneth watched the man pointing to the side and followed his line of vision to the very familiar curves of his wife's ass as she disappeared behind the hidden doors of the restroom area. Kenneth returned his gaze to the strange man and watched as the man continued to watch what belonged to Kenneth with a hungry look in his eye.

Time to put this shit to an end.

Kenneth walked over to the two men and took the only remaining free seat next to the stranger. "See something you like?" Kenneth asked with a false smile plastered to his lips. It was his business smile, the one he'd spent years perfecting to keep the sharks in the business world from ever knowing what was really going on behind his blue eyes.

Kenneth saw Bryan prepare to speak, but he lifted a finger to silence him. He so wanted to hear what this man had to say about his wife.

"Hell yes," the man laughed as he took a sip of his beer. "She's wearing uniform pants; you know what that ass must look like naked if it can make dress blues look like lingerie?"

A muscle in Kenneth's face ticked slightly. He leaned in closer to the man. "That's impressive. You know her?"

The man shrugged a shoulder. "Only through work, just met her today," the stranger laughed. "But after this work thing is done, I definitely plan on getting a piece of that."

Kenneth watched as Bryan nearly choked on the sip of beer he was trying to swallow.

"You all right, Smyth? Did I say something wrong, don't tell me you and Searlington are together?"

Bryan's eyes widened even more and he shook his head quickly. "Ah...me and Captain

Searlington...nah man, you're barking up the wrong tree."

"Good then that means I can take a crack at her," the stranger said.

"A woman built like that...I'm sure she's got someone waiting for her at home," Kenneth added.

"She might, but trust me friend, a woman as strong and powerful as that probably has some dude on a leash she bosses around all day. A woman like that needs a real man to reel her in and give her what she needs."

"Wow," Kenneth said quickly. "And I'm assuming you're just the kind of man that she needs."

The man rubbed his hands together and smiled a big toothy grin. "Oh yeah."

Kenneth watched the smiling man reach for his beer and take another healthy sip.

"Well, how about we make a little wager?" Kenneth asked. "You get her to show a little interest in you, and I'll buy your next round."

The arrogant man lifted his half-empty beer glass in salute to Kenneth and swallowed. "All right, friend, you got it."

Kenneth just smiled. He glanced over at Bryan who had a sort of panicked look on his face. Kenneth smiled again trying to defuse Bryan's tension. There was no need for concern. Kenneth was many things, but a jealous asshole wasn't one of them. He didn't have to be when it came to Heart. Just the thought of how her body molded to his cock kept him secure in the fact that everything about her was his and there wasn't another man made that could fuck with that.

Kenneth felt the familiar tingle in his spine that always told him his wife was near. He turned around on the barstool and smiled as the woman who owned him turned the corner with a full smile that Kenneth knew was only for him. She moved closer to him until she stood between his open legs. He snaked a hand around her waist and pulled her into him. He pressed her into his embrace and nipped at those glorious lips that he loved tasting.

He heard her moan, the only invitation he needed to deepen the kiss. He licked inside to taste the warmth of her mouth. She tasted like her favorite minty gum with a hint of spice from something she was likely eating before he walked in.

"Missed you," she said.

Kenneth smiled up at her. "Missed you too. You ready to go?"

She nodded. "Let's go inside and tell Porter and Willie we're leaving."

She stepped back out of his grasp and looked at the stranger sitting next to him who was staring at them with an open mouth.

"Weaver, this is my husband, Kenneth Searlington. Babe, this is Agent Weaver, he's working with us on a new case."

Kenneth nodded and smiled at the man. "Pleasure meeting you, Agent Weaver," was all he said before he stood and directed his wife toward the private room in the back of the diner. He knew he didn't have to say another word, the way Heart had plastered herself all over him already said everything Agent Weaver needed to know. She was unavailable to anyone but the man who had his arm around her. The last thing Kenneth heard before the door closed behind them was the howling of Bryan's laughter.

CHAPTER 7

*K*enneth walked into their master bath and turned the Jacuzzi jets on. He stripped down to his boxer-briefs and walked back into the bedroom to find his wife sitting on their bed. She looked tired and weighed down, but he was sure he knew how to fix that.

He knelt before her and removed the shiny patent leather uniform shoes from her feet. He peeled her black dress socks down off of each foot then he reached up for her belt. He made quick work of unbuckling it, and opening her pants. He pulled the hem of her white captain's shirt out of her pants and began unbuttoning it from bottom to top. When the flaps of her shirt fell apart he pushed it down the length of her toned arms then removed it.

He pulled her closer to him and let his lips softly press against the beat of her pulse in her neck. This was one of his favorite spots to touch on her body. Every time his lips met this spot he could feel how much her heart raced at the simplest of his touches. He continued to nip at that spot while skillful hands unclasped her bra. He pulled the straps down her shoulders and kissed the spot where the satin straps had touched.

He applied a small amount of pressure to her shoulder with his hand and she softly laid back on the bed. He kissed her lips, and continued to kiss the invisible line that traveled from the sensual extension of her long neck, between the deep valley of her mouthwatering breasts, down the flat expanse of her lower abdomen. He briefly tongued the cavern of her navel and hooked his fingers inside of the waist of her pants and panties.

She lifted her hips and he slipped the material down the rounded curve of her broad hips and toned thighs. He stood to admire his work and bit his bottom lip. If he tasted her again the tub might over flow which would suck all of the sexy out the air and he'd be stuck cleaning up the wet bathroom floor.

Bypassing that option he extended his hand to her and pulled her up on her feet with a gentle tug. He led her into the bathroom and lifted her into the deep and wide tub. When she was submerged into the bubbling water, he stepped in behind her. Once seated, he wrapped his wife in his arms and pulled her back against his chest.

Simultaneously they let out a collective sigh of relief. Skin-to-skin connection between them always brought about a soul-deep relief for both of them. He waited for her to relax in his arms before he started a sensuous stroke up and down the curve of her neck with his fingertips.

She barely stirred; he looked down to see if she'd fallen asleep. After the day she'd had it wasn't quite out of the realm of possibility.

"Hey, you still with me?" he asked quietly.

She drew a small smile on her lips to acknowledge his question.

"No," she answered in almost a whisper.

He looked down at her, a quick beat of concern marring his brow. "You alright?" he asked.

"Yeah, just tired," she answered. "I've been putting in a lot of work and time at the house on these prostitute murders. I think I'm just pushing myself a little too hard. It will pass."

He looked down at his wife. Her lids were heavy; they usually were when they were soaking in the Jacuzzi. But something just seemed a bit off. There seemed to be an added weight tightening her usually relaxed features. Maybe it was the work? Her job was less physical than it had been when they'd met two years ago. She didn't spend much time in the streets anymore, a fact he thanked God for every day.

He ran his finger over the rigid patch of scar tissue that rested on her right shoulder. Two years had passed and his insides still pulled in a painful contraction when he thought of how closely he'd come to losing her. She'd almost died in his arms because she'd been shot in the field.

When his godfather delivered the news that Heart would be promoted to captain, Kenneth's soul had danced. Yes, even in her role as captain she sometimes found herself in harm's way. Gladly, those occurrences had steadily declined over the last two years. Most days she was stuck in her office, reading, writing, and filing the paperwork that kept her precinct running. If it wasn't for the fact that she carried a badge and a gun, her work day would mirror his. She was safe inside of a building filled with other officers who would lay down their lives to protect her.

But there was something off; she was stressed, more than her usual load of paperwork brought. The skin just under her eyes looked a shade darker than the rest of the reddish-brown hue that covered her body.

Maybe it was this case, she was under so much pressure to solve these horrific murders that were plastered all over the evening news. Maybe she just needed some down time to relax?

Maybe she needed a chance to get away from it all for a few days?

"You look like you could use some time off. Why don't you take a couple of days and we'll find some little island to relax on."

She shook her head slowly. "I would love to, but with three unsolved murders, one of which being the governor's aide, there's not a chance in hell of me being able to get away."

"I don't like seeing you this way. You need to relax," he murmured against her temple.

"I will relax when the case is over, right now, I can't think of anything other than working this case so I can get brass off my ass." She snuggled deeper inside his embrace and allowed a soft woosh of air to spill past her pursed lips. "I'm afraid that if it doesn't involve working this case, or solving this case, I can't really entertain talk of anything else at the moment."

Those words washed over him like cold water on an already frigid day. Maybe now wasn't the best time to bring up kids after all?

She took another deep breath, easing it in through her nostrils, blowing it quietly out through puckered lips. "The only rest I'm going to get is the few hours we spend in that big bed of ours or here in this big ass tub with you."

He smiled with his lips pressed against her ear. "Well I guess that's good," he mused.

She turned her head just enough to raise one droopy eyelid in his direction. "It's good that

I'm so zonked out of my mind that I can hardly see straight?"

He nodded, "Yeah, because maybe you're so tired that I can get you to agree to anything I want and you won't remember it."

"Sweetie," she moaned. "You just drew me a bath in our Jacuzzi, you can pretty much get me to agree to just about anything right now."

He wrapped his arms around her, giving her a tight squeeze from behind.

"Good," he said. "Because I like having my way with you."

"Having your way, or getting your way?" she asked.

He spread his arms across the edge of the tub and shrugged his shoulders. "Either way, same result...I'm happy."

She rested her head on his chest and lulled back into the warmth of his body. This was how he would keep her every moment of every day if he could. Relaxed, open, free from worry, this was how she should always be. Now if only he could find a way to keep her that way.

She stirred just a bit and he continued to stroke her, trying to lull her back into relaxation, but she snaked a dripping hand into his hair, pulling him down for a sensual kiss.

"You're tired," he said when their lips parted.

"Never too tired for this, for you."

She turned around, facing him, pressing soft lips to his as she straddled his lap and swirled her hips in a slow figure eight motion over his semi-erect prick. Just a few more strokes against her mound and he would be at full mast.

He looked up at her, soaking up the radiance pouring off of her. This was his woman, his wife, and possessing that knowledge made him hunger for her the way a starving man craved food.

He fastened eager lips onto hers and grasped both cheeks of her ass with a firm grip. He pulled her down onto his aching flesh and savored the heated warmth of the contact. She swiveled her hips lightly and within seconds he was resting in the fire of her cavern.

"Mmmm...baby," he moaned and let his eyes drift closed as his head lulled back against the edge of the tub. There was nothing better than feeling of the tight as sin fit of her pussy squeezing the life out of his cock.

She tightened her walls in a sweet spasm and he had to bite down hard on his bottom lip to keep from losing his shit so soon.

"You keep that up and this is going to be over quicker than you'd like." She laughed and leaned in for a slow kiss, lapping at his mouth.

"Maybe I want this over quick, I mean, I am the one that has a.m. roll call at ass o'clock in the morning."

He slid his hands up her sides until his thumbs caressed the soft flesh of the underside of her breasts. He circled the heavy globes completely with eager hands and grazed the tight peaks of her nipples with his thumbs. He felt the electric shock his fingers generated through the shiver that passed through her body and down to her core. The quake causing her muscles to contract in the most deliciously tight grip around the throbbing length of his cock.

He lapped at one chocolate peak and then the next, savoring the sweet taste of the buds on his tongue. He sucked hard on them until he could feel the familiar quivers of her channel signaling her impending orgasm.

He surrounded her with his arms and leaned back as far as he could in the tub, lifting her bottom just slightly out of the water. He landed a hard smack on the wet skin of her ass and then soothed it with a slow loving touch before looking up and allowing the hungry lust he knew rested in the gleam in his eyes.

"Go for what you know, baby."

There was a brief moment that passed between them, a slight sliver of challenge that flamed in her eyes. He recognized that look, he'd seen in too many times not to recognize it. It was hunger, desire, and it was all for him. The very fact that he knew this woman wanted him with an equal passion that matched his own fire spark for spark made his balls ache with such a heavy need to release.

She slid back down his length and rolled her hips in the most torturous motion that made his toes curl and his feet search for purchase. God this is going to be an amazing ride. He braced himself for each snap of her hips and let her edge him closer and closer to his completion.

Usually he would have set out to make certain she came first, hell, he usually made sure she had at least two orgasms before he even neared his first. But on nights like this, when she had that fire in her eyes, he let her take what she wanted how she wanted it. Besides, he could tell from the vice like grip she had on his dick that she was about to explode with him.

He grabbed her buttocks and pulled her down onto him, his need to rut up into her driving the motion of his hips beneath the water. He could feel the water waving in fluid motion around them, the bubbling pressure of the jets tickling his taint, edging him closer and closer to the explosion he knew was waiting just outside his grip.

Wet fingers gripped his shoulders then moved down to his chest. She trapped one nipple and then the next between the thumb and forefinger of each of her hands and pinched the peaked flesh into a grip that was just this side of painful. He let out a deep howl as his senses finally found the thing he was missing, the thing he needed to reach. It was that amazing sensation of something hurting so good that his senses couldn't differentiate between pain and bliss.

He felt the muscles in his thighs, groin, and buttocks contract into that first glorious spasm that seemed to hold him in locked suspension. He felt her walls collapse around him in that familiar tight grip that formed to the perfect shape of his swollen dick.

He grabbed her to him and held on as their bodies flexed and relaxed repeatedly until they were both left spent in the bubbling water of the Jacuzzi.

She snuggled closer into his embrace making his currently flaccid cock twitch with thoughts of getting hard again.

"I think we might have made a mess on the floor with the water from the tub," he whispered quietly in her ear.

"Right now I'm feeling too good and too tired to give a damn," she slurred against his neck.

He smiled; he loved her this way, so fucked out of her mind that she didn't care about anything except enjoying the pleasure only he was capable of giving her.

Who needed ego stroking when you had a woman like Heart MacKenzie Searlington stroking your cock just the right way. His mind swimming in the blissed-out, sex-induced haze she always left him in every time they made love. There really was no describing just how invincible he felt when his woman slumped against him in a limp lump of erotic exhaustion right after she came all over his cock.

～

*H*eart sat in her office typing away at the endless reports on her computer screen. This was the thing that sucked most about her transition up the promotion ladder. She'd hated paperwork as a lieutenant. She had literally cursed Porter every time he'd handed something else to her to fill out. But as a captain, the paperwork that required her attention seemed ten-fold whatever she'd been doing two years ago when she was sitting at Bryan's desk.

This shit sucked, but she was captain, and she had an entire house of people depending on her. These forms kept her precinct running, kept her officers paid, kept her streets safe. So she stood up to refresh her coffee, and then she intended to dive right back into the bottom-less pile of work waiting for her.

She tipped the glass carafe over her empty mug and was in mid pour when she heard a tap on her door. She glanced back at the work on her desk then returned her sights to the door. A tap on her door never lead to anything good. Other than Bryan, no one dropped by just to say "hi' when you were captain. If someone was seeking entry, there was more shit for her to do waiting on the opposite side of that door.

"Yeah," she bellowed as she leaned down to take a sip of the strong coffee. It wasn't as nice as the stuff Kenneth made for her at home, but she was in a precinct, shit wasn't supposed to always be nice here. Besides, the familiar bitter brew usually stomped on her fatigue and gave her just enough energy to finish her tasks for the day.

Detective Grazzo leaned his head in the door. Now she knew some shit would drag her attention away from her desk, he never came in here unless he had something to show. Now she understood how Porter had felt as her superior officer when she was an eager detective.

"What's up, Grazzo?"

"We just got some new intel on the Silverson murder. L.T. sent me to get you."

She nodded and followed the detective into the conference room. She sat on the side and let Bryan run the show. Her job was just to listen and instruct when necessary.

"Apparently this girl had a lot going on," Grazzo began. "We were having a hard time getting into her laptop and digital files. Even her phone was locked tighter than the Pentagon.

She had military type encryption on all of her electronic devices."

"Were you able to get in?" Bryan asked.

"Not at first," Grazzo answered. "It took the I.T. team a minute to get past all of her security measures. There wasn't much of a personal nature on her devices, but she did have her calendar on her devices and there was something interesting. For the last three months she's had an entry in her calendar that simply read Rockaway and Pitkin.

We checked it out; there are only a few stores over there. No one had seen her, except for the last place we checked, a small free clinic that caters to the neighboring population."

"What was she doing there, volunteering?" Bryan asked.

Santini jumped in. "No, we think she was a patient there. We can't get the medical staff to confirm it, not with privilege and all that. They said if we came back with a warrant they'd give us specifics."

"Why would a woman who's an aide to the governor need to go to a free clinic? She must have health insurance," Agent Weaver queried.

"For anonymity," Heart murmured. "Places like that usually take folks without insurance. They work on a sliding fee scale, free for those that can't pay, minimal cost for those that can. She could have paid them cash out of pocket. Going through her insurance might have alerted someone she didn't want to know that she was seeing a doctor."

"We may not need her medical records," Detective Jenson offered as he pushed into the conference room holding a set of folders in his hand with Detective Ramirez behind him.

"M.E.'s report on all three victims," Jenson beamed as he walked to the table and handed the files to Bryan.

"Silverson was about fourteen weeks pregnant," Ramirez stated.

"Any clue who the father was?" Detective Thomas queried.

"No, the M.E. is running the DNA of the fetus through the system to see if they can find a paternal match. So far no go, she said she should know more by the end of the day...hopefully," Ramirez added.

Bryan handed the Medical Examiner's reports over to Agent Weaver. "So Agent Weaver, do you think this is the same guy you've been looking for? Do we have a serial killer in Brooklyn?"

Weaver scanned through the reports quickly with his finger. He stopped when he found what he was looking for then handed the files back to Bryan.

"No, I don't think so. Silverson, Grey, and Fernando were mutilated very similarly to the other victims, but they're all missing two crucial details. They weren't raped, and there was no number seven carved into their labia. Those were details we never released to the press," Weaver said.

"So whoever killed Silverson is a copycat?" Jenson asked the agent.

"Or he wants us to believe he is," Detective Grazzo offered.

Heart stood up, she'd heard enough, her second and his team were on the right track. "All right, Grazzo, I like that idea. Get us some proof to back it up," she said to the enthusiastic detective.

"Another thing, I know brass wants us to focus on Silverson, but she isn't the only dead victim in this case. There has to be something that connects her to the other victims. This free clinic might be a place that would see patients like our dead prostitutes. See if the other two victims were patients there as well. Do we have a lead on Silverson's mysterious benefactor yet?"

"No," Santini answered. "Computer geeks are still tracking the money."

She reached for the door handle and took one last look back at the detectives sitting around the conference table. "Find him," was all she said before she exited the room just as quietly as she'd entered.

CHAPTER 8

*K*enneth sat at his desk getting absolutely nothing done because he was too busy thinking about his wife. He missed her, ached for her, and until he could put his hands on her, his mind was for shit at focusing on anything but the imprint of her body on his.

He couldn't function this way. They'd both been pulling relentless amounts of hours at their respective offices, sacrificing time with one another to fulfill the demands of work. His head understood it, but damn all that, he missed his woman and he was about to do something about it. The police commissioner could kiss his pale ass for all he cared; tonight he was going to spend a regular night at home with his wife on the couch watching whatever mess they had on their DVR.

He picked up his cell phone and swiped his finger across the idle screen. He pressed a thumb against her smiling face and waited for the call to connect. It rang three times, once more and his call would be sent to voicemail. He was waiting for her greeting when he heard a strange and male voice click on to the line.

"Who are you?" Kenneth asked.

"Ahh, you called this line, don't you think you should be telling me who you are first?"

Kenneth sat up a little straighter in his chair. There was something almost familiar about the sound of the man's voice talking shit to him on his wife's phone.

"Well friend, there are two very simple reasons why your assumption is wrong. The first, I pay the damn bill for this number, so I get to ask whomever picks up this phone other than the person that's supposed to who the fuck they are. And second and most importantly, this number belongs to my wife, so if you aren't her, you'd better have a damn good reason for answering her phone. Now I repeat, who the fuck is this?"

There was a beat of silence before Kenneth heard the other man's voice crawl over the line. "This is Agent Weaver, Mr. Searlington. Captain Searlington just stepped out of her office for a moment on police business. Would you like me to give her a message for you?"

"None that I need you to deliver," Kenneth's cool voice replied. Whatever else the agent was about to say never registered past the click of the ended call. Kenneth scrolled through the contacts on his phone until he found the number he was looking for.

"Smyth," Bryan said after the first ring.

"Bryan, is Heart with you?"

Bryan must have heard the urgency in Kenneth's voice because he sidestepped all of the banter he'd usually throw Kenneth's way whenever they spoke over the phone. "Yeah, hold a sec and I'll get her."

He waited patiently, his temper slowly boiling with each beat. He didn't know what this

Agent Weaver was playing at, but he wasn't in the habit of letting people fuck with what was his in business or his personal life. He was going to nip this shit in the bud right now.

～

*B*ryan gave Heart a strange look as he handed his cell phone to her.

"It's your husband, and he doesn't seem very happy," Bryan whispered. She took the phone and put it to her ear.

"Hello?"

"Where the fuck is your phone?"

She pulled the phone away from her ear and looked at it, then looked up at Bryan who just sort of shrugged and stepped away from her giving her some privacy for her call.

"Kenneth…everything okay?"

"Where is your damn phone, Heart?"

Okay, she thought. She turned around looking for the hidden cameras trying her best to pick them out of her surroundings. She couldn't see them, but they had to be around, because there was no way her man was raging on the phone at her otherwise, this had to be a joke.

She took a calm breath and answered Kenneth's question.

"Bryan and I went to the pizza spot on Crescent and Sutter to get some lunch; I forgot my phone in my office. Is everything okay?"

"No, tell that agent that's hanging around your precinct to stay off your damn phone. Don't let me call my wife again and that fucker answers."

Heart raised her hand defensively and stepped out of the tiny pizzeria so she could speak freely. "What? He answered my cell phone?" she asked. "You sure you didn't accidently dial my office phone?"

"Heart, I've been dialing your numbers long enough to know the difference between the two. I don't appreciate that shit. You'd better check him before I do."

Heart rolled her eyes at Weaver and her husband. Yeah, Weaver had overstepped, but that didn't really warrant the reaction that Kenneth was storming through right now.

"All right, I will, but why are you coming at me this way? Is something else going on?"

"No, just check him. See you tonight when you get home."

The line clicked, the called ended, and she stood looking at the phone.

"What was that about?" Bryan asked as he walked out of the pizzeria with boxes of steaming food.

"The fuck if I know," she said as she as she turned toward her dark blue sedan. She opened her door and climbed inside waiting for Bryan to do the same.

She pulled out of their parking spot on Crescent, made the left turn on Sutter Avenue and started sailing quickly toward her precinct.

"You know, if you're going to drive this fast through residential blocks you might want to switch on your lights and sirens," Bryan offered through smiling lips.

She mumbled a quick "fuck you" under her breath and continued her quick pace until they were pulling into the precinct parking lot. She stomped through the back doors of the building structure and headed straight for her office.

When she stepped inside she found Weaver with his feet up on her desk reading something from his tablet. She slammed the door shut and gave his locked ankles a hard shove, forcing him to sit up correctly in the chair.

"Did you answer my personal cell phone?"

The agent looked at her carefully, she presumed he was trying to gauge just how angry she was or wasn't.

"Yeah, I did."

"Why?"

"It was ringing, and I thought it might be important so I answered."

"Don't ever answer any of my phones again, business or personal. That's what voicemail is for, if it's that important, the caller will leave a message."

"Your husband didn't sound happy on the phone."

"That's an understatement. What did you say to him?"

"Nothing, told him you were out for bit." Heart peered at the agent with suspicious eyes.

"You had to say more than that. Kenneth is usually sickeningly calm. He doesn't normally let people get under his skin. What did you say to him to piss him off like that?"

Weaver sat there and shrugged his shoulders innocently. There was something that wasn't right about this scenario and she would find out what it was.

"Listen to me very carefully, Agent Weaver," she said. "I know you secret-agent types are usually cagey and plotting to stay five steps ahead of everyone else. But trust me when I tell you, don't fuck with me and mine, I promise you'll regret it if you do. We understand each other?"

She crossed her arms and waited quietly for his response. He stood from his chair and gave his head a slow nod.

"Perfectly, Captain," he replied.

He turned and left the office, leaving her a fuming mess and she didn't quite understand why.

She heard the click of the door and saw Bryan walking through the door with their food in hand. *Good, maybe I'm just pissed because I'm hungry.* It sounded like a good enough excuse in her head.

"Everything all right?" Bryan inquired.

"Yeah...no...I don't know," she hissed.

"This have anything to do with the very angry husband that called my phone?"

She looked at Bryan considering if she should share her thoughts. She and Bryan were much more than boss and employee. They'd spent years as partners and he'd been her second when she was lieutenant and now captain of this house. He was her go to guy, but most importantly, he was her friend. Hell, a few years ago she'd even thought they'd end up as family if he married her cousin Justice as the Amare family assumed he would've.

She motioned him over to the table in her office where they sat opening boxes. If she were going to have this conversation, for damn sure it wasn't going to be on an empty stomach. She pulled out a hot slice steaming with bubbling extra cheese on a well-done crust. There was nothing quite like a slice from the pizza spot on Crescent and

Sutter. Toni and his people really did know their way around a brick oven.

She carefully bite into the stringy cheese and crunchy crust, quickly moving the piping bread around her mouth trying hard to balance her greediness versus her need to not have second degree burns on her tongue.

"So, remember when we got to the pizzeria and I realized I'd left my phone on my desk?"

Bryan nodded and she continued. "Well apparently, Kenneth called while I was out."

The investigator in Bryan sat up and he looked at her with a questioning side-glance. "So he was upset because he called you and you didn't answer? That doesn't really sound like something Kenneth would get mad over. He's usually the kind of guy that doesn't sweat the small stuff," Bryan added.

"No, Kenneth wasn't mad about the fact that I missed his call. He was mad because Weaver answered my phone."

Bryan stopped in mid-chew and placed his slice on the paper plate sitting in front of him.

"Shit, I told him to watch himself around Kenneth," Bryan mumbled.

"Why would he have to watch himself around Kenneth?"

She watched her second. He knew something, that was for certain, but whatever it was, it didn't really look like something he wanted to share.

"Bryan, if you know something, speak," Heart insisted.

The man ran his tongue on the inside if his mouth poking out his cheek as he chewed on more than just his food.

"Look Mac," he began, switching to his nickname for her. The shortening of her maiden name was a clear indication that whatever he had to say wasn't business-related in the least. "You know we'd all had a few that night we went to talk to Porter and Big Willie about this damn case?"

She nodded. The five of them had gone through quite a few pitchers of beer together. Kenneth had driven her home so she gladly took advantage of not having to be a responsible drinker that night. Bryan had stopped after one beer early in their night in order to drive Porter and Willie home. She wasn't quite sure how Weaver made it home, she'd been the first to leave when Kenneth arrived to pick her up.

"Well, Weaver was feeling pretty nice that night. I think the beer kind of went to his head. When the three of us walked out of the private dining area you went to the bathroom, and he and

I sat at the bar and ordered another pitcher for the table."

She nodded; she remembered these events just as Bryan was detailing them. She still wasn't certain what this had to do with Kenneth losing his mind today.

"Well, Weaver started asking me about you. What kind of person you were off the job? Were you into work liaisons of the personal kind? Before I could stop him he started making comments about your physique, how fine you were and all that. Just as I was about to interrupt him, Kenneth walked in. He must have seen how the guy was staring after your ass because he asked Weaver about it."

She rolled her eyes. *That's what this was over, some jealous macho bullshit?*

"So Kenneth went off on Weaver?"

Bryan shook his head. "No, he played it really cool, started egging Weaver on, making him think he was a friend, not revealing who he was. Even got Weaver to make a bet that he could get you to show some kind of interest in him. I mean honestly, it was genius, Weaver never suspected a thing. Thought he was coming off looking like a big man."

"Until I showed up five minutes later shoving my tongue down Kenneth's throat," she moaned.

"Yup, and let me tell you, Weaver was not happy after you and Kenneth left. He felt like Kenneth made a fool of him. I told him he was out of line and he couldn't be mad with Kenneth for staking his claim on his woman," Bryan added.

"Yeah, but if Kenneth got the upper hand, why is he beasting at me over a phone call?"

"Mac, it's not about the phone. Kenneth pissed a line around you that night letting Weaver know that whatever he was thinking he'd better rethink because you were his. He probably went home and forgot about it, but this dude answering your phone, a cat that he knows is into you, that would be enough to piss me off if I was in Kenneth's shoes. I mean, over the two years you and Searlington have been together, how many times have I answered your phone?"

She thought about Bryan's question. The truth was it was extremely rare for anyone else to answer her phone. The handful of occasions it had happened she'd been sitting right next to Bryan and had given him permission to answer it.

"You think Weaver is a problem?"

Bryan shook his head. "No, I think the guy just saw an attractive woman that he was interested in. He had one too many beers and let his liquid courage help him to shove his foot far down his throat. Cut the guy some slack."

She turned over Bryan's suggestion in her head.

"Was he really that drunk?"

"I don't know if I'd label him drunk, he wasn't falling down or acting crazy. He was just buzzed, felt good, and thought he'd take a chance. That's all," Bryan answered.

Heart heard a tap on her door and answered with her customary, "come in." Detective Grazzo walked in with a folder in his hand and an excited look on his face.

"Cap, L.T.," Grasso greeted them both. "We've got the financial records back from Silverson's school." He walked over to the table and spread the folder and its contents between the two senior officers.

"All her tuition and personal bills it seems were paid with accounts belonging to a Q. X. Tivé," Grazzo offered.

"Who the hell is this? What's this person's connection to Silverson?" Bryan asked.

"We don't know yet, L.T. The I.T. team is trying to figure out who this person is. They say so far they can't really find much info other than a few accounts that were being used to support Silverson," Grazzo answered.

"Alias?" Heart inquired.

"That's what we're thinking. I.T. is still digging to try to get us a real lead on this person," Grazzo responded.

"Good work, Grazzo," Heart commented. She collected the files and handed the folder back to Grazzo dismissing him. When they were alone again, she turned to Bryan with a lifted brow.

"The rest of your team had better be careful. Soon enough, that boy is going to be a sergeant and your second in command," Heart commented.

Bryan nodded. "If the poor fool knows like I know, he'll stay the hell away from that sergeant's exam," Bryan added.

"Regretting taking that lieutenant's exam, Lieutenant Smyth?" Heart asked with a genuine smile tugging at her lips.

"Every fucking day of my life since," Bryan offered.

"Those words seem vaguely familiar." Heart let out a laugh and blocked the balled up paper napkin Bryan threw at her.

～

Heart snapped her head up at the rapid succession of loud thuds against her office door.

"Cap, we gotta lead," Smyth uttered quickly as he popped his head in her office doorway and turned right back around into the hall.

That was not a good sign. Bryan was the most laid back individual in life and if he was barking into her office, something significant had to have happened. She jumped up, grabbed her sidearm and jacket and headed toward the team conference room.

"What's up?" she asked as she walked into the room. She gave the room a quick glance; all members of the team were present and accounted for, including Agent Weaver. Her stomach did that little anxious twirl it had started since the beginning of this case.

The swirly buzzing in her gut wrote a reminder memo in her

inner notepad. *See doc to make sure this fucking case hasn't given you an ulcer.*

She swallowed, trying to push the nausea aside, reaching in her pocket for a stick of mint gum. She wasn't much of a fan of things of the mint variety, but mint was the only thing that seemed to calm the churning in her stomach and keep her from spilling her guts literally across the conference room table.

I swear I gotta put this case behind me. "What do we have, Smyth?"

Bryan handed her a folder as she walked to a seat at the conference table. "Ramirez and

Santini were able to get some information last night from the working girls on Ho Stroll."

Heart didn't speak, just waited for the team members to jump in.

"We were able to get some of the pros in the area to talk to us about the working girls that were killed," Santini added. "Those two girls were new to the scene on Ho Stroll. Apparently, the two prostitutes were pimped out by Roman Medrano, local businessman and hustler."

Ramirez jumped in, "Medrano has a couple of legitimate businesses on file that help him clean the money he makes from girls on the street. According to the girls on Pitkin Ave, girls start out at Medrano's gentleman's club as dancers; he then manipulates them into working at his so-called escort service where he attaches the girls to his VIP clients that can afford the finer things in life.

As long as they stay in popular demand, and are obedient, they stay with the escort service.

If they fall off for some reason, or make the mistake of pissing Medrano off, he busts them down to walk his streets on Ho Stroll. Both these girls just showed up on the Ave a few weeks before they were murdered."

Heart nodded her head, soaking in the information the detectives were providing. "Well that can't be a coincidence," Heart stated. "Two of his newbie streetwalkers are killed within weeks of arriving on the scene. What do we know about Medrano, and his businesses?"

"If you're asking if there's anything in his past or present that will give us probable cause to walk up in his places and inspect them, the answer is yes," Bryan offered.

She smiled; they were so in tune with each other's thoughts and practices at work that he knew exactly where she was headed without her having to speak a word.

"He pissed off one of his hookers," Bryan continued. "Arlene Yates, former 'Top Bitch,' her words, was replaced by a younger model and turned out on to the streets. He told her the only way she could get back into the club was if she brought in to some new meat."

"That sounds like the beginnings of a racketeering charge to me. Who do we plan to send in as the new meat?" Heart asked as she looked down into the file and perused the typed pages in her hands. As she read, the unusual pause in the conversation pulled her attention from the file in her hand to her subordinates sitting around the table.

All eyes were on her and instantly the reason clicked in her mind as to why. "Hell no."

"Come on Cap," Ramirez answered. "You and L.T. have the most UC experience out of all of us."

"That may be true, but I'm also the ranking officer in this fucking building. I don't know that brass would take kindly to one of their captains shaking her ass in strip club." She shook her head. "I think I will leave this to you guys to figure out Detective Ramirez."

"Mac," Bryan's familiar use of her name pulled her away from the staring war she was having with Ramirez at the moment.

"I can't send Ramirez in, she's been all over the crime scene, and she's been on Ho Stroll relentlessly canvassing and interviewing witnesses. They would make her."

"Bryan, I'm not the only female cop in this damn building. Find someone else?"

"No, you're not. But the rest don't have your experience and everyone that does know how to run an op like this is either otherwise engaged, or is just not right for the part."

Heart rested her ankle over her knee and shrugged her shoulder. "What's that supposed to mean, right for the part?"

"Captain Searlington," Weaver interrupted. "I think what you're officers are trying to tell you is that you are one of the few women that know how to do the job, and possesses a body fit enough that you wouldn't be laughed off a stripper's stage."

Her gaze scanned the room finding agreement in every set of eyes seated at the table. She took a deep breath and closed the folder in her hand, placing it none too gently on the table.

"Why the fuck did I become captain if it wasn't going to keep me from prancing around a stage in a G-string?"

CHAPTER 9

"*R*emind me again why the fuck we're here in a strip club in Brooklyn versus closing this damn deal in our office?" Kenneth barked at his friend sitting beside him in the car.

"You know the answer to that," Alan answered. "We're dealing with an idiot that actually believes most business deals are closed in places of ill-repute. I tried to get Shaw to see reason, but he insisted that we come down here to have a little fun while we wrapped up business."

Kenneth gripped the steering wheel, angry heat rising up from his tightened fists through his arms and finally seeping throughout the rest of his rigidly coiled body. He took a breath and struggled to relax himself. He couldn't let himself short-circuit yet. This deal was too important for him to lose it over that power-tripping asshole Shaw.

"Ken," Alan reassured him. "Just let this buffoon have his moment. Sign these fucking papers and make yourself a shitload of money. And when you're done, make sure to place a hefty cut of it inside my bank account and we'll both forget about this idiot."

Kenneth's fingers loosened around the wheel and he turned to his friend and laughed. Moments like this always made him cherish the easy friendship he and Alan had. Kenneth nodded his head, Alan was right, he'd be a fool to lose this deal worth hundreds of millions just because he couldn't stand being in the same room with this particular buyer.

He opened the door and Alan followed suit falling in rhythm with his steps toward the door to the strip club. Kenneth paid their entrance fee and asked for a table in their VIP section. A young woman, blonde hair, light eyes, in the darkness of the room he couldn't really tell the exact color. She was slim with a tiny pair of black lace boy shorts on. She had a matching halter that was barely holding the straining expanse of her heavy bosom at the moment. He cocked his eyebrow and gave Alan a knowing glance. When they were in college, they definitely would have attempted to take a woman like this home.

"Welcome to Gentleman's Delight. My name is Treasure and I'll be your server for the evening," she smiled as she leaned in closer to speak to them. Kenneth wasn't sure if it was because the loud music made it hard to hear, or if she was just trying to boost her tips by giving them a better viewing advantage of her tits. Deciding it was probably a combination of both, he returned her smile. "Can I get you gentlemen something to help you relax after a long business day?"

"Yes," Kenneth answered. "...what kinds of high-end scotch do you have at the bar?"

Kenneth watched the smile beam on Treasure's face. Depending on what they had stocked, a rare bottle of scotch could cost upwards of ten thousand dollars. Gratuity on a bottle like that, and Ms. Treasure's month was probably made.

"Well that depends on how high-end you want to get," she answered with a tilted smile.

"The best you have in stock," Kenneth replied.

"We have a nineteen fifty-five highland single malt scotch, it runs about fifteen grand," her cheeks warmed from the pale rose of whatever kind of blush she was wearing to a deep mauve. Apparently hefty price tags were her thing. Who would have guessed it in a place like this?

Kenneth shook his head, and removed his black card from his wallet. He placed it carefully on her server's tray and watched as her eyes widened with what he could only described as a cartoonish-like quality. Just looking at her made him ache for his wife. Before Heart, this type of money-grubbing individual would have been the type of company he sought. It was funny how life changed when you met the right person. Now, the only thing he longed for was the tall mocha beauty that lie in his bed every night.

"I'm going to need to see some I.D. to complete the transaction," Treasure added.

He nodded and pulled out his driver's license. She glanced at it and smiled. "Thank you Kenneth," his name slid from her suddenly pouty lips on a sultry breath. "Can I get you anything extra?"

Kenneth took his license back and gave her a knowing smile. "No, my wife gives me all the...extra I can handle."

Her shoulders pulled up in to a defeated shrug, as if she were saying, "You know I had to try, right?" She turned around and moved toward the bar.

"Make sure you add your twenty percent gratuity on to that charge my dear," Kenneth called out to her. The disappointment left her, twenty percent of fifteen grand was going to be a sizable tip, and if the extra jiggle in her hips was anything to gauge by, Treasure had just done the math and was very happy with her calculations.

Kenneth found the entire exchange amusing; he really wasn't bothered by her behavior. It wasn't like he hadn't spent most of his life dodging opportunistic people who only wanted to associate with him because of his money. He was used to people eyeing him like he was the prized fatted calf on the table, but he'd learned the hard way that people like that often used you up and then spit you out.

No, Ms. Treasure was a beauty, but she wasn't shit on a stick compared to the woman who wore his ring and carried his name.

He pulled his mind away from the fiery thoughts his mind was concocting about his wife and focused on the business at hand. He just wanted this night to be over. The near twenty grand he'd just plopped down was to serve one purpose only—stroke Shaw's immense ego, make this damn money, and get the hell home to his baby. She was probably leaving work headed toward the house now. As far as he was concerned this damn meeting couldn't be over quick enough.

Shaw just rubbed him the wrong way. It wasn't that Kenneth didn't like being wealthy, he could floss with the best of them, but for him, he never believed his money made him better than anyone, and that was Shaw's fatal flaw as far as Kenneth was concerned. An expensive damn bottle of scotch should not define you, but Kenneth knew that twit, Shaw, would be excited that Kenneth had laid down that kind of cash for a bottle the three of them could polish off in a matter of minutes if they were serious drinkers.

"Two glasses," Treasure said as she sat two thick tumblers carefully down on the table between him and Alan.

"Four glasses, we're waiting for friends," Kenneth replied.

"More devastatingly handsome men, I must have done something good to get such a treat."

Treasure walked away toward the bar to retrieve two more glasses and Kenneth and Alan just shook their heads as they laughed. The show she was putting on was definitely nice, but the truth was, his desire was longing for Heart, no one else.

Kenneth looked around the dimly lit room. The club itself was somewhere near the BQE in a developing part of Brooklyn that was filling up with a variety of new businesses. Successful business people from Manhattan were moving into Brooklyn just across the bridge for the lower cost in real estate. It was really genius as far as business models went. They were close enough to Manhattan that all of the people with money could patronize them, but the business paid lower rates on everything from real estate and zoning costs to inventory. Cutting expenses and increasing profits was what business was all about, and in this particular instance of gentrification, you ended up with an upscale gentleman's club in Brooklyn that sold fifteen thousand dollar bottles of fifty-five-year-old scotch.

Kenneth shook himself out of his thoughts and allowed his gaze to pan his surroundings. It was tastefully decorated. If it weren't for the women in various stages of undress, this place really could have passed for a chic lounge or restaurant.

Kenneth saw the subtle move of his companion's head and took notice. With a discreet gaze Alan alerted Kenneth to Shaw's entrance into the club.

"Time to put your game face on man," he encouraged. "An hour or two, and you never have to see this fool again."

He was right, all Kenneth had to do was smile and bullshit his way through the next hour and he would be rid of this flashy idiot. Kenneth opened the scotch and poured himself and Alan more than two fingers. Hell, if he didn't have to drive he'd pour the whole damn hand. By the looks of the grinning simpleton walking toward them, they were going to need it.

Shaw, accompanied by his lawyer, sat down at their table wearing a smug smile.

"Kenneth, Alan, you fellas ready to make an obscene amount of money?" He slapped Kenneth on the back and Kenneth had to grind his teeth to keep from throwing the closed fist that rested on his lap.

"Shaw, sit down man," Kenneth added through a forced smile. He poured a healthy dose of the amber liquid in a glass and handed it to the man. "Let's celebrate."

Shaw smiled and swallowed the scotch in one gulp. Kenneth laughed, a drink like this was meant to be savored, but Shaw was too busy trying to make a show of everything he nearly choked himself trying to finish the glass in one swallow.

"Damn, that's good," Shaw barked between raspy breaths. "Tastes like money."

Kenneth nodded and took a sip of his own drink. *Just keep playing the role and this will be over soon.*

"Well gentleman, let's say we get down to business so we can enjoy the show," Shaw beamed.

"Show?" Kenneth asked.

"Yeah, every Friday night they have a newbie perform on center stage. I don't know how the owner does it, but each week the new chick is finer than the last. They've been promoting this new girl through their email list. Diamond is supposed to be her name. If her pictures are anything to go by, she's the hottest piece of ass I've seen in this place in a long while."

Kenneth didn't particularly care, after these papers were signed, he was headed straight for his wife.

"Well then, let's get this business finished up so you can enjoy your show," Kenneth remarked as he handed Shaw a shiny new pen and pushed the first of the documents in Shaw's direction.

~

"*J* am so gonna kick your ass when all of this is done," Heart growled through the tight set of her jaw as she glanced over and watched her second's shoulders shake with laughter.

They sat in a blacked out SUV getting fitted with surveillance equipment. Bryan sat in the bucket seat next to hers in the second row while Agent Weaver and Bas Arroyo sat in the driver and front passenger seats. The surveillance tech squatted in front of her and creatively attached the smallest microphone she'd ever seen to the skimpiest outfit she'd ever worn. *I have lingerie that has more material than this floss I'm wearing now.*

"Okay, Captain," the tech uttered. "You're all done. This baby will pick up a whisper a mile away. Just speak normally; you don't have to worry about increasing your speech volume in order to be heard on tape."

Heart nodded and scooted out of the way while the tech left the four of them in the vehicle alone.

"You ready for this, Searlington?" Agent Weaver asked.

She lifted her eyes to him. She found concern there, the same expression she'd seen in Bryan's eyes over the years whenever they were working undercover.

Anytime you walked into the enemies camp there was always a certain level of risk. Walking into the unknown always left any law enforcement agent vulnerable. But she was a veteran at this point, she knew how to stay safe and stick to the plan they'd agreed upon. Heart was the talent, Bryan was her pimp, and Arroyo and Weaver were his muscle. Together the four of them would try to find out what they needed to solve these damn murders.

"I'm good, Weaver," she confirmed. "All I have to do is dance."

Bryan shook his head, "MacKenzie, don't take this shit lightly, you've done this before. I don't think any of us like the idea of you going in there without your sidearm."

She understood their concern, but it was what it was.

"I'm wearing floss Smyth and four-inch glass slippers," she quipped. Seeing the deadpan expression on all three of their faces she knew she wasn't winning any arguments with the sarcasm, "Look guys, I'm here because you all said it had to be me. I'm the head of this team and I know what I'm doing. As long as you all do your jobs, I'll be fine. Are we ready? I really need for this to be over."

She popped her ear wig inside her ear canal and watched as they all three mirrored her action. They tested them, and when they were all satisfied that all their tech was in proper working order they exited the vehicle.

Bryan came around the back and held a long coat open for her, protecting her from being exposed. Weaver and Arroyo led the way and Bryan held out his hand for her to take it. She knew this would be the last time he asked permission. The moment they walked into this club, she was his property, if they couldn't sell that, they could end up dead...or worse.

When she took Bryan's hand he pulled her close to him and planted his lips hard on her mouth. She didn't even fluster, they'd done this before, she wasn't Heart Searlington, she was a stripper named Diamond and this was her handler.

She allowed Bryan to open her mouth and deepen the kiss. As the kiss continued she felt Bryan slip something small and sharp into the slight pocket of space the rested between the skin on her hip and the tiny leather micro panty-shorts she wore. As soon as the object was secure he ended the kiss and captured her face in a harsh grasp between thumb and forefinger.

"If you're separated from us or if shit goes bad..."

She nodded her head and ran a discreet finger over the object. He turned her around, and they headed into the club.

Game on.

CHAPTER 10

S haw had just signed the very last contract and Kenneth felt a gush of relief with the last twist of Shaw's wrist. The deal was done, and Kenneth didn't have to lay eyes on this fool ever again. Well...maybe again if he wanted to purchase another ridiculously priced property.

Kenneth packed up the signed documents and poured the last of the scotch in Shaw's empty glass. Kenneth and Alan were still nursing their first and only glass. Picking up a DUI charge when your wife was a captain in NYPD was a no-go, so he'd sipped his way slowly through only half his drink.

Kenneth raised his glass, "To Ian Shaw, may you enjoy your very expensive new digs."

Shaw brightened and took another large gulp of scotch from his glass. Kenneth shook his head and moved his tumbler toward his lips when a familiar tingling traveled down his back and spread through his chest and limbs.

He turned quickly, looking for the one individual that was responsible for it. His eyes quickly spanned the club, but in the dark, he couldn't make out any faces. He saw a cluster of people move from the door disappearing quickly behind a dark velvet curtain, but he couldn't make out any definitive features.

He was about to stand when Shaw's lawyer asked him something. He half listened and half searched the club for the only person in the world that was connected to him on such a visceral level that he could actually feel her walk into a room.

He tore his gaze away from the dark curtain and focused on the lawyer and what he was saying. The music increased several decibels and the dim lights became outright dark. There was a loud announcement over the mic that Diamond had finally arrived and the applause in the club became deafening. Kenneth didn't even turn toward the stage; he just wanted to end this meeting and making it home to his wife.

Kenneth leaned in closer to hear what Shaw's attorney was attempting to say. When he could finally piece the question together, he answered the man. The crowd began to get downright unruly with their catcalls, banging their hands against the tables and screaming for Diamond. Kenneth heard an unmistakable, "Oh shit," coming from Alan. It sounded like a whisper in the raucous noise surrounding them, but if he'd heard it at all over this noise Alan had to have been screaming it.

Kenneth looked over at his friend and saw his mouth hanging open with a matched pair of broadly set blue eyes focused on the stage. He followed the path of Alan's fixed gaze. His curious stare climbed the stage from the floor to familiar russet-brown skin on legs he knew from sense memory alone. His eyes continued up to the most perfectly curved hips followed by the sensuous valley that had called to him from the very first moment he'd had the chance to lay eyes on it. His vision traveled up and across a torso stacked with the most perfect handful of round flesh a man could ever want to touch or taste. He closed his eyes, so afraid to let them take the final few inches up. Once he saw her face, he would have to admit that this nightmare was really happening and it wasn't just his overactive imagination.

He cracked his lids open and let them crawl those last few inches until they were resting on the most beautiful face he'd ever seen and his heart dropped into his stomach. There on that stage, in nothing more than a few scraps of leather to cover the more essential portions of her flesh, was his wife, Heart.

His breath caught in the center of his chest and he lifted a shaky hand to try to soothe the ache. He didn't remember standing up; he briefly heard Alan call his name and realized he was standing over his friend. Alan was saying something, but Kenneth couldn't make out the words. He sidestepped the hand Alan stuck out in his path to halt him. He moved with fixed resolve toward the stage not registering the angry calls of those he pushed past to get to his destination.

By the time he made his way through the crowd of rowdy patrons screaming for more, and begging for her to show more skin, the song blasting through the speakers was over and she was making her way to the end of the stage. He finally locked his gaze on to hers as she looked over her shoulder. There was something wrong. The usual connection, acknowledgement they shared wasn't there waiting for him. It was like she was another person, not his Heart at all.

He went to step closer to her when a tall black man dressed in a black leather jacket and shades and a dark colored fitted cap put his arms around her. He drew her into his embrace and placed a possessive hand across her ass, pulling her into greedy kiss.

Kenneth's vision clouded with crimson.

That motherfucker is going to die today.

～

*B*ryan released his captain from the kiss he'd just placed on her lips. Anyone looking would think she was his, that's the story they were selling, that's what they needed people to believe.

He and MacKenzie were very good at what they did, it's why they'd both sailed up the professional ladder and ended up in command of the seventy-fourth so quickly in their careers.

They absolutely rocked at this UC shit; problem was they'd never anticipated that her fucking husband would walk into the middle of one of their ops. *Shit.*

He moved his lips to her ear; they looked like two lovers enjoying a secret moment together.

"We've got a problem," he whispered.

"I know," she answered.

"You stay here with Weaver, Arroyo and I will take care of the issue," he informed her. He gave her a quick smack across her ass and moved in the direction of the seething man barreling toward them. He nodded to Arroyo to follow him and within a few steps they were standing in the path of what looked to be a man with murder in his eyes.

Just what I fucking need, my fucking boss' husband ready to beat my ass.

Before Kenneth could speak, Bryan clapped a hard hand on his shoulder and turned him in the direction of the door. When he seemed to put up some resistance, Arroyo stood in front of him and discreetly flashed the piece that was sitting in the waistband of his jeans.

Bryan saw Kenneth's friend stand up from their table. *Ethan, Eric... Alan? Yeah, Alan, that's his name.* Bryan took off his shades and locked eyes with the man, hoping he would recognize him and realize there was no reason to come to his friend's rescue.

Bryan returned his hard gaze to Kenneth. He could see the internal struggle warring within Kenneth. The brief hesitation allowed Bryan to direct Kenneth toward the door and out of the club. He pushed him into the back of their SUV and turned away from him to close the door behind them. When he faced Kenneth again he caught a hard fist to his jaw.

Kenneth drew back again and got one more wild shot in before Bryan subdued him in his seat with a forearm across his throat.

"The fuck is wrong with you, Searlington?" Bryan howled through his aching jaw.

"Me?" Kenneth responded. "You had your fucking hands and lips on my fucking wife."

"Kenneth man, calm the fuck down," Bryan advised.

"Calm down? How would you like it if you walked into a public place and found me pawing your woman?"

Bryan was a bit puzzled by that question, especially since this was MacKenzie's husband.

"My woman?" Bryan shook his head and focused on the man seething with rage under him. "Kenneth, are you gonna let me explain what you walked in on, or am I going to have to cuff you to the fucking seat?"

Kenneth nodded his head and the wild look in his eyes died down just enough that Bryan surmised it was safe to release him. Bryan sat back into his chair and rubbed the throbbing spot on his jaw.

"Damn man, you hit fucking hard."

"Just because I sit behind a desk doesn't mean I can't defend what's mine."

Bryan nodded his head. "So noted. Look man, you know damn well nothing has gone on between Mac and me."

Kenneth looked at him through slotted skeptical eyes.

"I thought I knew that, Bryan. But then I walked into this club and see my wife shaking her ass on stage half naked and you pawing her like she's your fucking property."

Bryan ran a rough hand down his face, trying his best to remember the man flexed and ready to punch him again was a friend.

"Exactly, Kenneth," Bryan answered. "Your wife, my boss, was shaking her half-naked ass on stage and let me, her second in command, shove his tongue down her throat and smack her ass. Does that sound like the MacKenzie you know?"

Kenneth watched him. Bryan could almost feel Kenneth's cold blue eyes passing over his features, assessing and seeking the truth. He took a ragged breath in and when he pushed it out, all of the poised tension he held in his body dissipated and he fell back into the bucket seat.

"Shit, you're working."

Bryan nodded his head. "Yes, Kenneth, we're working, and if you had gone any further you could've blown our cover. There are some very dangerous people in there, and we need to make this shit look real. Can you deal with this? Or do I have to leave you in here cuffed to the door?"

"Bryan, I don't—"

"Kenneth, quite frankly, I don't give a fuck what you don't like or want. I don't have time to play this nice, so I'm going to give it to you straight. Right now, Mac and I are playing a role and if you can't bear to watch it, get the fuck out. The cover we have is necessary. She and I will do whatever we have to in order to sell it and keep all of us safe. So if I have to fuck your woman in front of you to keep those bastards in there from getting suspicious and killing her, then that is what I will do, and you will sit back and watch it and not say a fucking word.

"Right now, instead of being in there protecting her, you got me and Arroyo out here dealing with your crazy ass. Weaver is great, but who would you rather in there with her, some agent we all just met, or someone who's had her back since before you did?"

He watched Kenneth, hoping what he'd said had sunk in, and hoping it hadn't gotten him fired. Mac understood police work, but she was just as blindly protective of her crazy ass husband as he was her.

Slowly the man nodded his head and brought his temper under control. He wasn't happy. Who would be under the circumstances? Bryan knew this was a fucked up situation, but Kenneth loved his wife, and he wasn't about to endanger her any more than necessary. At least Bryan hoped he wouldn't.

They exited the car and met up with Arroyo who was standing outside keeping watch. When they reached the door Bryan caught sight of Alan as he walked up to them.

"You all right, man?" Alan asked Kenneth.

"He's fine, and to make sure he stays that way, make sure he gets home safe," Bryan added and walked off inside the club. Hopefully that was the last of the excitement he had to deal with tonight.

*K*enneth nodded at his friend to let Alan know he was all right. He pushed back into the club intending to collect his belongings and get the fuck out of this godforsaken hell hole. He glanced around for his wife and her team, but he couldn't find any of them. She was still here, of that he had no doubt. He could still feel her, as if she was standing next to him.

He arrived at the table and caught sight of Shaw filling out some kind of slip and handing it to their server, Treasure. Shaw looked up at Kenneth with a smile dipped in filth.

"You want in?" he asked.

"In on what?"

"Whenever they debut a new girl here, they run a high-stakes auction. Whoever wins gets a special dance with her in the middle of the dance floor and they get some alone time with her in one of the back rooms behind those velvet curtains over there."

His heart thudded against his chest at the thought of other men having their paws on her. There were several problems with this scenario. Heart had learned to work with her issues with touch over the course of their relationship. She was able to manage the uneasiness, but it still made her uncomfortable. He also wasn't that thrilled with the idea of the lecherous patrons of this club spending money to get their damn hands on his wife. That shit was not happening.

"How much is the buy-in?"

"Ten grand," Shaw answered.

"What's the top bid you've seen win?" Kenneth almost growled as the words left his mouth.

"Fifteen to twenty grand," Shaw smiled again. He rubbed his hands together in conspiratorial way, like he was celebrating bringing Kenneth into his lame ass fold. "You like her? I never knew you liked dark meat, Ken."

Kenneth's hand tightened into a fist in his pocket. If the safety of his wife wasn't on the line he'd like nothing more than to plant all of his fucking weight into the bastard's sickening mouth. Instead, he looked up at Treasure and took the blank slip she was handing him.

Once he'd filled it out. She gave him a paddle that was marked with an identifying number, told him bids were only collected in cash, and wished him good luck.

"If you don't walk with that kind of money Kenneth, I can spot you," Shaw offered.

Kenneth's face stretched out in tight lines. "No worries, I got this."

Kenneth pulled out his phone. It was hours after the end of the banking workday. At this time of night banks were closed to usual customers. Fortunately having the president of the largest bank in New York on speed dial placed him in that *special* customer category. Being ridiculously wealthy had its benefits. Getting his hands on unbelievable amounts of cash whenever he wanted was one of them.

He pulled out his cell-phone and texted his banker with his request. After a series of security hurdles the two had in place to make certain this was actually Kenneth attempting to gain access to his money, Kenneth received a confirmation text that the money would arrive via armored guard in thirty minutes.

He caught Treasure's attention as she attended to another table. He pointed to the empty bottle of rare scotch and nodded for another. She smiled in acknowledgement and he sat back trying to sit on the explosion that was threatening to break free of the barricades he'd thrown up.

When the bottle arrived, he poured a steady amber stream into his glass and sipped slowly. He needed to be calm, not drunk, so he took his time and let the warmth of the scotch trek through his system and take the edge off of his rage.

Kenneth sat there for what seemed like forever, waiting for this show to get started. He pretended to entertain the bullshit Shaw was talking, but in truth, he was forming his tactical plan.

He saw his banker walk in with a metal briefcase in hand flanked by two burly men dressed in black. He knew from experience that the case was shackled to its carrier's hand. That money was going nowhere until Kenneth gave the okay.

The lights came up just a little and the music in the room fell silent. Kenneth watched a Latino, possibly Mediterranean, man take center stage with a microphone.

"Gentleman," the stranger began. His words colored with a mix of Spanish and Brooklyn. "Y'all know what time it is? It's time to find out who gets to spend a little quality time with our newest edition, the lovely Ms. Diamond."

The crowd went up in cheers and applause. Kenneth took a large swallow of his drink. He had to keep his anger chained. Otherwise, this entire charade was going to go tits up.

"So, the bidding starts at ten grand. Which one of you will give me ten grand to spend time with Ms. Diamond?"

Kenneth saw Shaw's paddle go up and several quickly followed upping the cost to thirty grand. Kenneth lifted his paddle and called out, "Fifty thousand."

All heads turned toward him, including Bryan who'd just entered the room from that velvetcovered doorway. If looks could kill, he'd be dead, but he didn't give a fuck. This was his wife, and he wasn't about to let this shit go down. Not when he could do something about it.

The man on the stage smiled wide. He walked to the side of the stage and held out a hand. Kenneth watched as Heart took the offered hand and walked onto the stage. Long chocolate legs sauntered across the stage from one end to the other and turned to twist the sexy curve of her hips in an enticing dip.

She knew what the fuck she was doing, she was baiting him, and it was working. His cock twitched with the knowledge of what those magnificent hips were capable of.

"We got fifty grand. I don't know about y'all, but I'm sure that ass is worth more than that. Anyone willing to give me fifty five, or is the gentleman in VIP going to be the lucky winner tonight?"

There was a beat of silence and someone else agreed to bid the fifty-five thousand. Kenneth's eye twitched. No way was he losing this bid. Men kept raising their paddles, fewer than in the beginning, but still too many for Kenneth's taste. He raised his paddle again.

"One hundred and fifty thousand," Kenneth bellowed.

The entire room went up in noise. Things were getting interesting now. When the auctioneer asked for one hundred and fifty-five, the participants dropped down from a handful to just two, Kenneth and another man sitting on the opposite corner of the room.

The stranger raised his paddle and agreed to the new amount. Kenneth raised his paddle and upped the ante by ten grand. The two men went back and forth until the latest bid was a hundred and ninety thousand dollars.

Kenneth was honestly tired of playing this game, it was over, and he was walking out with his wife. He took the last swig of liquor in his glass, crossed his leg, and sat back comfortably.

He raised his paddle slowly, and called out, "Five hundred thousand dollars." The entire room went silent.

"My man, you do realize this is a cash auction. No checks or credit allow," the man from the stage called out.

Kenneth nodded and left his paddle remaining in the air. He waited while the man on the stage asked for more from Kenneth's opponent, but the man simply laid his paddle down, and conceded.

"Going once, going twice...sold to the gentleman in VIP."

Kenneth rested his paddle on the table and locked fiery gazes with his wife. She was his, and everyone in this fucking room would know it.

⚯

*H*eart took a shaky breath when Kenneth was announced the winner. She didn't know if she should shake him or thank him, he'd both saved her and thrown a monkey wrench in her investigation as well.

She stepped toward the end of the stage and waited as he offered a helping hand to her. She took careful steps down the stairs and felt the burn of the skin of his hand connecting with the her palm.

When they reached the center of the dance floor she heard the first straining beats of Trey Songz "Na Na." By the time Trey asked if they were fucking tonight, she and Kenneth were grinding against each other with determined movements.

God, the slide of his body was making her clit throb with a nasty ache. She needed this fucking assignment to be over so she could slide down the beautiful cock that was currently pressed up against her resting perfectly in the fissure of her rounded ass.

He placed one strong hand flat against her abdomen while the fingertips of the other skated down the length of her arm until she felt blunt fingertips, caress hers locking their fingers together in a beautiful latticework of brown and cream digits.

He pressed his mouth to her ear and the warmth of his breath seeped through her skin and into her blood, igniting a chaotic boil inside her. He nipped at her ear and whispered one word that made her forget about all of the people watching them, the operation, and anything else that didn't directly relate to the fire he was stoking between them.

"Mine," was all he said and her mind blanked out, and all she knew was him: her man, her husband, her anchor.

This moment wasn't about the case, it was about the way the two of them connected, had always connected, on a primal and visceral level. She fell into step with him and let him lead her around that dance floor. His moves were powerful and made her ache to be beneath him in their bed, or up against a wall. Either would do at this moment, she just needed this man.

He turned her to face him; she plastered herself against him, his thigh between hers, her riding it trying to get more friction. Just a little more pressure and she could probably fall over the edge into bliss. Just a little more…

She felt herself fall back. Kenneth anchored her by keeping a secure grip on her neck. She leaned into it and let her body shake, dip, and roll against the solid strength of his body. God she was there, just a few more movements of her hips and she could find completion. She was a horny, craven bitch tonight, and she didn't have one stitch of shame about it.

She felt him pull her back to him, burying his face in her neck, and kissing his way back up to her ear.

"I could fuck you right here. And I bet you would let me," he surmised. "I can tell how close you are right now." He held her tighter, changing the angle against her clit, removing some of the pressure. "No, not here," he said and her body trembled with want. "I will not let the people in this fucking room witness the beautiful sight of you coming for me. That shit is mine and mine alone. You're going to finish this fucking thing you've got going on tonight, then you're going to bring your ass home and let me bury myself so deep in this fucking pussy you'll be walking gingerly for the next week."

He bit down on the sensitive flesh that covered her shoulder forcing another involuntary shudder to charge through her body.

"Do you understand me?"

The music stopped then. With glaring silence filling the room, she was able to find the will to shake her head free of some of the fog Kenneth had poured over her mind. He held tight to the back of her neck forcing her to stand in the full onslaught of his powerful gaze. She realized then that his question hadn't been rhetorical, he expected an actual answer.

She wrapped her arms around his neck and placed a gentle kiss on his cheek and whispered one word in his ear.

"Yes."

He ran his hand across the expanse of one of her ass cheeks and gripped it firmly, making certain his stamp of ownership would remain there long after this dance was finished. He nodded his acceptance of her answer. He looked over her shoulder and nodded, and then he stepped out of her embrace.

He plastered that cocky ass grin he'd been wearing when she'd first met him. The one that said, "I'm certain I'll be fucking you soon," then turned and walked out with Alan in tow. If she didn't love him so damn much, she was sure she could hate that man.

She stiffened as the haze he'd created cleared her mind and she came to a startling realization. *Dammit, the fucking mic was on to my earwig the whole fucking time. Shit, I'm fucked in so many ways.*

CHAPTER 11

*H*eart had never finished debriefing and writing up post-mission reports in her life. She wrapped up the loose ends and knocked on Bryan's office door to let him know she was on her way out. When she poked her head in the door he looked up and waved her in.

"You outta here for the night, Mac?"

"Yeah, gotta go home and see what kind of mess is waiting for me."

She watched as his knowing brown eyes danced with mischief. His lips bent into a smile that barely hid the laughter he was holding back.

"I think we all know what's waiting for you at home. I've always known Searlington was protective of you, but tonight I found out first hand just how much."

"He is possessive, but never like this. I think him seeing you kiss me took him to a place he didn't know how to handle. He should have known I was working the minute he saw me on that stage."

Bryan shook his head. "That would have required him to think rationally, Mac. Tonight wasn't about him being rational. Tonight was all about how he felt. Tonight, he felt someone was tarnishing something of his. If I'd have walked in on the same scene, I'm not sure I wouldn't have done the same thing."

She nodded her head, taking in what Bryan was saying. It was true, what Kenneth walked in on would have been too much for a saint. The fact that he'd lost it a little tonight, well, she couldn't blame him all that much.

"Did we catalogue all of the evidence we collected tonight? How many did we end up bagging for prostitution charges in the rooms behind the velvet curtain?" Bryan did a quick perusal of a sheet of paper on his desk.

"We picked up Madrano and five of his associates. We also picked up about ten girls in the back and eight Johns."

"You think we can get any information out of Madrano?"

"I think if we let him stew tonight and come back at him in the morning, we can probably get something useful out of him. Go home to your man, make him feel better and don't step back in this place before noon tomorrow."

She laughed at the irony of her lieutenant giving her orders. As funny as it was, it wasn't even all that uncommon. Bryan had always looked out for her, and apparently her increase in rank wouldn't change that.

"Mac, the boys in the tech lab told me they'd keep certain parts of the audio as quiet as they could."

She rolled her eyes. "Bryan, I'm not about concealing evidence. I'm not ashamed about anything regarding my relationship with my husband. Kenneth and I had no idea the other would be in that club. Hell, I didn't even make any arrests tonight. I was just a distraction; you guys did all the work."

He nodded his head. "That may be true, but…"

She waived a dismissive hand. "Bryan, it's fine. I know, I'm supposed to be NYPD's golden girl. A tape like that could tarnish my image, and fuck with my ability to be taken seriously. I get all of that, but the truth is, I could give a fuck about all that. All I really want is to be a cop and do my best to protect this city I've been given command over."

He nodded quietly; there was nothing either of them could do about the tape anyway. As bad as the unedited tape probably sounded, it would be worse for all involved if they tried to cover it up. Transparency was key.

She pushed her hands inside of her fitted trench coat. She was about to turn toward the door when she heard Bryan call her name.

"You're still wearing that little leather two-piece you were dancing in tonight, aren't you Mac?"

She didn't even have the decency to be ashamed at the grin that was spreading across her face.

"There's only one man who will ever know the answer to that question, Smyth. And he's waiting for me at home."

The sound of his laughter chased her out of his office all the way to the parking lot exit at the end of the hall.

She hurried down the hall, eager to get to her car when she heard, "Captain," coming from behind her. She turned to find Agent Weaver in a light jog trying to catch up with her.

"You needed something, Weaver?"

"Yeah, I'll be headed back to Florida chasing my favorite serial killer. I just wanted to tell you it's been a pleasure getting to work with you and your team."

She nodded, watching the pregnant look in his eyes. "Anything else, Agent?" she asked, certain in the fact that Weaver had stopped her for something other than the, "it was nice knowing you," kind of thing.

His eyes dropped just a little, before he finally lifted them to meet her gaze.

"I'm sorry," finally crossed his lips

"For?"

"For speaking out of turn with your husband at the bar and on your phone," he answered. "I was out of line. I should not have ever gone there. Thank you for not making an example of me because of my foolishness."

"Weaver, you do damn good work. The rest of it, well, that's not really important. Safe travels," she said as she extended her hand.

He shook it, and retreated down the hall the way he'd come.

She made it to her car as quickly as the skinny heels she was wearing would carry her, a happy smile dancing across her mouth as she jumped into the car and started the ignition. She was on her way to her man, and if the last few hours were any indication, she was in for a world of hurt. Hopefully the good kind.

The drive home was quick, partly because of the late hour, mostly because of the lead foot she had pressed against the accelerator. In less than twenty minutes she was pulling into her driveway. She took a moment to look at their house. It was completely dark, matching every other house in the quiet Long Island cul-de-sac where they resided.

Maybe he went to sleep; maybe he's put all of the bullshit from tonight behind him.

She quietly turned the lock and quickly punched in the security code to their alarm. The house was still, yet another clue that Kenneth was probably sleeping. She took off her spikey stripper heels and padded softly across the carpeted floor toward the staircase. When her big toe touched the first step she heard the familiar baritone of his voice surrounding her.

"I hope you're not ready to retire already, wife."

She tried to move the thick ball sitting in the dry cavern of her throat. She forced a hard swallow and turned her head toward the living room. A soft click and then the room filled with a soft glow of light coming from the small lamp bedside the couch.

She turned from the stairs and walked around to the living room, where Kenneth sat in the same clothes he'd left the club in. She expected rage when she finally stood in front of him. Instead she found an unnerving calm and control resting over his entire body. He was sitting there, legs crossed, tie loosened, glass tumbler in his hand with a small amount of tawny liquor covering its bottom.

"Everything all right, baby? I thought you'd be asleep by now."

His face was impassible, smooth, devoid of any tension. But there, in the depths of his azure eyes she could see the storm raging with electric streaks of fiery lightening flashing with passion.

"Kenneth—" she never had the chance to finish her sentence. He stood up quickly and grabbed the front of her trench coat and pulled her to him with a sharp tug.

"Not a single word. I want you to go upstairs, secure your weapon, and come down to the basement. Don't go to the bathroom, don't take your coat off, just lock up your gun, and find your ass in that basement now. Do you understand me?"

The chill in his voice made her nipples tingle and spine straighten. God the things this man could do to her, and he hadn't even touched her yet. She nodded her head and watched him turn and leave the room in the direction of the basement. She was still stuck there a moment later when she heard his voice in the distance.

"Trust me, Heart, tonight is not the night you want to keep me waiting."

She snapped out of her trance and ran up the stairs. She locked her weapon away and within seconds she was barreling down the stairs and heading toward the basement door.

When she opened the door there was silence, not even the sound of him breathing. She found him in the home theater. He was sitting in the middle of the front of the four rows of leather seats that declined from high to low as you walked into the dark room. When she was finally in front of him she opened her mouth to speak, but he silenced her with a single finger.

"You don't need to explain anything," he said softly. "This isn't about punishing you because Bryan had his hands on you or the fact that you were putting your pretty little ass on display in that club tonight. I know you were working, I know you didn't have a choice."

She raised a brow. She was confused now; if his actions hadn't been about his anger at the scene he walked into, then what was all this?

"Tonight is about one thing and one thing only. This is about my need to exorcise this raging burn that has been threatening to consume me since I saw someone else's hands on you. So you are going to do everything I instruct you to do tonight until I rid myself of this need to beat someone's ass passes and I'm so sated with your body that neither of us can move from where we fall."

Her breathing was ragged, he hadn't even touched her yet and she was ready to fall in to a puddle at his feet. He moved closer to her, bending down and placing his face just out of range of kissing. He was so close she could feel the heat from his body licking at the meaty flesh of her bottom lip.

"Are you okay with everything I've said, with everything I intend?"

She and her husband weren't into the BDSM scene. With the exception of the few times she'd used her handcuffs on him or the times he'd used his silk ties on her...okay, so maybe they weren't as vanilla as most suburban couples, but they certainly weren't the type to put collars around each other's necks.

Kenneth was dominant by nature. He didn't yell and bang his fists against the furniture, but when he spoke with powerful quiet, he never left a doubt to those around him that he was running shit. It was the thing that had pissed her off the most when she'd met him, and the thing that turned her on the most now that they were married.

His asking her to acknowledge that she was granting him permission to do his worst, that was a clear sign he planned to lose all his restraint, all of his gentleness, and that thought alone caused her womb to open and close in anticipation of the things he had planned for her.

She took a slow breath and met his eyes. She knew if she didn't provide him with a clear and explicit answer he wouldn't touch her. That was not an option. Her skin felt tight and uncomfortable. Her muscles were restless, she needed his touch to quiet the electricity that was exploding across every hypersensitive nerve ending she had.

She took another breath and licked dry lips and nodded her head as she quietly said, "Yes."

He pressed a button on the remote in his hand and the curtains covering the wall-mounted LCD screen of the monitor slid back. Streaks of light from its screen began to fill the room and she could hear the recognizable bass of the of Ciara's "Ride" permeating the air.

He grabbed the coat again, and yanked them together until every part of their bodies touched, including their lips. He pressed closer to deepen the kiss, shoving his tongue inside her mouth. He grabbed a handful of her hair and buried his fingers into the dark strands. The sensation was overwhelming, pin pricks of excitement dancing against her scalp coupled with just enough pressure to make her pain receptors take notice.

He held her in place, positioning her just where he wanted her, taking his sweet time devouring her mouth. When he was finished, he ripped his mouth away. She could feel the redness of her burning lips throbbing in time with the pulse in her dripping pussy. *Whatever the fuck he wants, hell yeah I'm down.*

"Dance for me," he whispered just before turning away from her and returning to his seat.

It was like simple arithmetic. Kenneth giving her a subtle command and her fucking traitorous body just obeyed. She couldn't even remember how the sultry moves had begun, but her body of its own accord began twisting and rolling to the driving beats spilling out of the surround sound speakers. Thank goodness this entire basement was soundproof. All she needed was to have to explain this shit to the Nassau Police Department if a nosy neighbor dialed nineone-one.

She danced as she unbuttoned the trench coat that felt like it was smothering her. She threw it aside and allowed her hips to roll in controlled movements. She glanced briefly at the screen on the wall to see the dancers in the music video commanding their bodies to shift to the pulsing beat.

She looked back over her shoulder and caught a glimpse of her man sitting in the reclined chair, legs spread out adjusting what she knew to be more than a handful of skilled, strong, and long cock that she hoped he'd allow her to worship.

When Kenneth was like this, there was no guarantee that he'd let her adore him. Sometimes all he wanted was to take care of her, see to her pleasure. She wasn't complaining about that either. The truth was Kenneth's hands on her always equaled explosive pleasure. But tonight...tonight she needed to revere his flesh.

She continued her movements, low-dipping hip rolls, body rolls, hair whipping from side to side as she danced for her man. She extended her hands to him begging him to dance with her. She needed to feel the press of his body against hers.

He obliged, moving slowly from his seat, he rolled up the sleeves of his dress shirt. When he reached her the video had changed to Pretty Ricky's "Grind on Me." He turned her around and pressed her ass into the curve of his groin and fastened biting fingers on her hips to make certain she remained there.

As the music and the lyrics dictated, they began a slow but powerful grind. He was so thick and hard against her. His body fluid with movement, but stiff in all the right places she needed him to be.

The dark curtain of his long hair fell over her shoulder and tickled the sensitive skin of her neck. She reached a hand up and laced her finger through the strands, loving the way they softly rubbed against her.

When her fingers touched his scalp he pulled his head out of her reach and whirled her around so that they were facing. He fastened his lips on her mouth in a punishing kiss. When he was done, he placed his lips next to her ear. "You're going to keep your hands to yourself tonight and I'm going to make certain of it."

He stepped away from her and removed the tie that was dangling loosely around his neck. He twisted the silk material in his hands as he stepped around her. The first touch of it against her skin made her shiver. The mood this man was in was going to end her.

He secured her hands behind her back. Her wrists bound, she tested the strength of the restraint, her breath catching when she realized she really couldn't break free. He must have been some kind of Boy Scout when he was a kid, because the motherfucking knots he had in that damn tie were professional grade. If she wanted to be free of the binding, she'd have to work for it...if she wanted to be free.

He stepped back in front of her, placing a gentle hand on her cheek. The gentleness of his touch was in vast opposition to the stormy cobalt fire that was filling his gaze.

"Are you sure this is what you want?" he asked, his lips thinned into a terse line.

She nodded her head and he gripped an aggressive hand in her hair, bringing a sharp pain that both thrilled and alarmed her at the same time.

"Speak," he said.

She took a breath and moistened her sealed dry lips. "Y-yess," she whispered.

"Knees," was all he said. His voice was calm and still.

If he'd been in any other situation, she'd have sworn he was having a normal conversation. Context was everything, because the flame burning in his eyes was anything but normal, everyday Kenneth.

She fell to her knees, no questions asked and waited for his next command. She watched him unzip his dress pants and pull himself slowly through the slotted opening. Discomfort painted his face. His cock was so rigid, standing straight up like a sword ready to pierce flesh, it was a wonder he hadn't damaged something pulling it through such a tight space.

He gave it one long stroke and pushed it against her mouth. She opened wide, granting him access and he shoved himself hard and fast to the back of her throat. Being with Kenneth these last two years had taught her to control her gag reflex long ago. The man was in no way lacking in the length and girth department, but tonight, her eyes stung and watered as the war to suppress her body's natural reaction to retch at such a harsh invasion.

He never gentled, just kept using her, fast hard strokes, his heavy sac slapping her against the chin, the bulbous head of his cock stabbing her throat. What a debauched mess she must be. She could feel tears streaming down her face, her nose running, and the heavy pool of saliva dripping down her chin to the middle of her neck and chest.

Her pussy was aching so much. The walls of her womb clenching in hard spasms, begging for something long and firm to hold on to.

He pulled from the warmth of her mouth just as abruptly as he'd entered it. He ran an abrasive finger over her lips and slowly knelt down next to her. He placed his hand at the base of her throat and helped her lie on her side on the floor. He moved slowly, unfolded himself behind her and pulled her into the heat of his embrace.

He removed the hand from her throat and used it to move her leather boy shorts to the side. He pressed a single finger inside of her, rubbing the pad of it across the crackling bundle of nerves on her anterior wall. She was so fucking hungry for him right now, she was sure if he stroked that spot just once more she would explode.

"No," he said as he pulled his finger away.

Breath caught in her chest, she turned pleading eyes on him.

"Not until you're on my cock, not until I say so."

He moved the leather aside again. She felt the heavy press of his cock against the dripping hole between her legs. She couldn't see it from this angle, but she knew the bulbous head had to be dark with blood turning the angry flesh from its usual pink to a furious shade of plum. He shoved inside of her, filling her in one brutal motion, the material covering his still clothed body scouring against her skin, making her cry out with need. The resulting moan that seeped out of her lips was equal parts pleasure and pain and she had to wonder for a moment when pain had become her fucking kink.

It didn't even matter, he was moving inside of her now. He hooked an arm under the bend of her leg and pulled it back until knee met her breast. He locked her leg in position by securing his hand around her neck and he pushed so deep inside her she feared she might split in two.

He pummeled the walls of her pussy, just battered them. Each stroke bringing louder unintelligible sounds that smacked against the walls and back to her ears, making her dizzy. She was so open, both emotionally and physically, and it was such a heady feeling, tripping over into a freefall that both scared and thrilled her.

He scraped against her G-spot again and the pieces broke apart ripping a full body orgasm from her. Her body struggled to convulse and pull away from the attack, but Kenneth held her in the same immovable position and barreled through her orgasm and her feeble attempts to pull away from him.

When she thought she couldn't take anymore, he lowered her leg halfway giving the straining muscles and ligaments a brief reprieve.

He cupped her head with his remaining hand and held it still while he plunged his tongue in her mouth.

His kiss was rough, the newly risen stubble of a barely there shadow of a beard abrading the skin of her face and chin. When he tore his mouth away she could feel the burning flesh of her lips throbbing in relief.

He pulled out and positioned her on her stomach. He pulled back on the curve of her hips and forced his thigh between hers, spreading her for him. A sharp sting warmed the flesh of her ass and she shivered, pressing back toward him, asking for more. He repeated the action, fire searing both inside and out, bringing her dangerously close to another explosive orgasm.

She felt his body cover her back as he leaned over her, burying deft fingers in her hair and pulled her head back to his ear.

"I wanted to hurt something, break something, when I saw Bryan's hands on you. You are mine, now and forever. No one else should know what you taste and feel like except me. I know

I can't stop you from doing your job, but I can damn sure make certain that if you're ever in the position again, the only man you're thinking of is me."

He threaded his remaining arm across her back and beneath her bound limbs, locking strong fingers onto her bicep. Her hands were effectively trapped between the crack of her ass and sexy as fuck lines of his muscular abs. He plunged inside of her setting up a severe pace. She was quivering, fucking pussy dripping enough to soak through the material that made up the crotch of his pants.

He was fucking her so hard she just wanted to splinter in to pieces. Afraid of the approaching climax and at the same time afraid he wouldn't let her cross it. His hands pulling harder on her body and in her hair, the nerves on her scalp singing with the most delicious pain.

She bit her lip to try to quell the scream building inside her.

"No, I want it, give it to me," he yelled and yanked her hair harder, diving into her with more force, grinding his cock so far inside her she was sure he was going to break something.

She couldn't take the abuse he was delving out, her walls quivering more in stronger spasms. Her moans turned to wailing screams leapt from her raw throat and she screamed her way through the most amazing climax she could ever remember having.

She felt his forceful speed sputter and knew he was about to follow her into bliss. He released her hair and wrapped his arm around her neck and pulled her back against his chest as he growled to completion.

He held her pressed to him for a few moments as he pushed and pulled ragged breaths in and out of his lungs. He loosened his grip on her, placing soft caressing touches on her breast and abdomen. He kissed the curve of her shoulder, calming her, soothing her after riding her so hard. He sealed his lips over hers enjoying the unique taste of them before he nuzzled his nose against her cheek.

"Mine," was the last thing she heard before her blitzed out mind clouded and the darkness swallowed what little light remained in the dimly lit room.

CHAPTER 12

*H*eart reached for the ringing cell phone in her pocket while her eyes remained glued to her computer screen. The tender muscles in her arms protested the quick, careless movement after last night's events. She still tingled and ached in all the places Kenneth laid his hands on her last night. She wiggled a little bit, trying to take pressure off of her sensitive ass. She'd have to remind him that the next time he wanted to play rough she'd need at least two days available for rest and recuperation afterward.

"Searlington," she nearly growled, annoyed at the interruption in her hard-won focus over her delicate lady bits and the damn files she'd spent her entire morning poring over.

"Captain, this is Le'Ticia Riggs. You got a minute?" the even female voice asked.

Heart and Leticia Riggs had worked very closely together through much of Heart's career. Usually eerily upbeat considering her chosen profession of working with the dead, Heart found a strange seriousness in the woman's voice.

She looked down at her phone and saw that Le'Ticia was calling Heart from her personal cell phone number. That wasn't the strangest thing in the world, I mean the number was plugged into Heart's cell because the two women did converse on occasion off the books, but something just didn't seem right. "'Ticia, everything okay?" Heart queried.

"I'm driving to you now," Le'Ticia said through the windy noises mixing in with her voice. "I'm about ten minutes from your precinct, but I'd rather meet you someplace else. Is there any place we could meet that wouldn't be crawling with eyes and ears from either of our offices?"

Heart thought for a minute. The diner was out of the question; too many of her cops frequented that spot. She thought about it again and came up with the perfect destination.

"Yeah, there's a spot a few blocks away, but still very isolated. Just park your car on

Glenmore and Essex. See you there," Heart ended the call and dialed her second's cell phone number from memory.

When she heard the familiar "Hello" on the line she instructed Bryan to meet her in the back, alone, ASAP. Within minutes they were in her car and driving the few blocks to their destination.

"Why'd we take your car to your pop's work? We could have walked these two blocks from the precinct," Bryan stated.

"Yeah, but I never leave myself without transportation when I don't know what I'm walking into."

They climbed out of the car and each popped the snaps on their respective holsters. Something about meeting for unknown reasons on this very isolated block that held nothing except the industrial warehouse-like building of her father's business made her uneasy.

She entered through the back entrance that was hidden by an alley and the overgrown bushes of the neighboring abandoned two-family home. When they reached the door, she pulled out a set of keys Marcus had recently given to her. She entered first and found her father sitting at his desk busy at work.

"Marcus?"

Marcus MacKenzie raised dark brown eyes to meet her face.

When he realized who'd called his name, he stood up and met her in the middle of his office.

"Heart, what are you doing here?" he asked, mouth smiling, obviously happy to see her in his space again.

Over the last two years she and Marcus had worked diligently to bridge the fourteen-year gap that had torn a gaping hole in their relationship. She'd forgiven him for actual and imagined grievances, but the path to a traditional father-daughter relationship was long and windy, filled with all sorts of traps and stones to trip you up along the way.

She braced herself for the slight touch to her shoulder she knew Marcus would apply. It was his usual greeting, one they'd worked hard to figure out. Slowly but surely with the help of her husband and her therapist, she was learning more and more to distinguish between good touch and bad touch. In the short span of two years had even learned to welcome touches from those she loved.

Hi, Marcus," she returned his smile, "I hope you don't mind me dropping in unannounced. I needed someplace discreet to have a conversation."

"Discreet," he echoed. "Hope that's not a euphemism for sneaking around on that son-in-law of mine?"

Bryan stepped into the office and extended an offered hand to Marcus. "Not as long as I'm tagging along. Kenneth is my dog."

Marcus took the offered hand and shook it with zeal. "Always glad to know there's another set of eyes looking out for my daughter's best interests. How are you, Bryan?"

"Good, sir."

Marcus turned to Heart and spread open arms. "So what's going on, Heart?"

"It's work related. I'm expecting someone who asked for a discreet place where we could have a private conversation. Can you spare your office for the next few minutes?"

Marcus nodded and walked toward the door. "I'll be out front taking care of some things. Let me know when you're done."

She nodded her thanks and met her second's questioning gaze.

"Dr. Riggs from the M.E.'s office wants to see me. She said she needed a place where official eyes and ears were scarce."

"What did she want?"

Heart raised her shoulders in answer. "Not sure, but it sounded like it was important. Can you go back out the way we came in and bring her back here? She should be pulling up any moment."

Bryan nodded and went in search of their expected visitor. She studied the white walls of her father's office and laughed to herself. "I swear I'm going to buy you a bucket of paint and get rid of these walls that have been staring back at you for the last thirty-some-odd years, Marcus."

Just as she finished her perusal, she saw Bryan fill the doorway, then step aside for Le'Ticia to enter the office. She was an African-American woman of average height and build with dark strands of straight hair that was cut in to a short bob hairstyle that kissed the soft angle of her jaw.

"'Sup, Doc? What's with the cloak and dagger routine?" Heart asked.

Le'Ticia's dark eyes usually danced with a playful intellect that shone behind her thick lashes. Today, her eyes moved swiftly back and forth and she quickly focused on pulling a folder out of her shoulder bag and handed it to Heart.

She pressed the folder into Heart's hand. "I found out something from Ms. Silverson's pending autopsy test results that I didn't want to chance the wrong person finding out about over the phone."

"Ticia, what's going on? You almost look scared."

The woman tucked her hair behind her ears and stared at Heart. "That's because what I have to say could cause a great deal of trouble. Do you remember a few years back when you busted that serial rapist?"

Heart nodded. "The one who almost raped the mayor's daughter? Yeah, why do you ask?"

"Well, although she wasn't raped, we did run a rape kit on her because you guys caught the guy literally with his pants down. We took hair samples from her current boyfriend at the time to rule him out as the possible donor for the pubic hair we found on the victim's thigh."

Heart remembered the details of the case. The governor's son and the mayor's daughter were dating at the time. The young man was actually a standup kid, he volunteered against his father's advice to provide them with a hair sample in order to shut down the defendant's claim that the hair came from the vic's boyfriend and not him.

"What's that got to do with the reason you wanted to see me today, 'Ticia?"

"Because I ran the DNA of Silverson's fetus and today I found a match."

Heart felt the blood rushing in her ears as realization took root. "Are you telling me the governor's kid is the father of Ms. Silverson's baby?" Heart questioned.

Le'Ticia shook her head. "No, I'm telling you that Ms. Silverson's unborn fetus and the governor's son share a father."

Heart looked at Bryan and saw the same wide eyes she knew were bulging out of her own sockets. She looked down into the folder to read the official report sitting in her hand and instantly understood why Le'Ticia didn't want to talk about this over their office phones. If information like this was mishandled then it could decimate several careers, namely the governor's, and theirs.

Heart took a deep breath and snapped the file closed in her hand. "Fuck my life."

❧

*H*eart and Bryan sat in an unmarked patrol car behind the postal facility at the end of Fountain Avenue and waited for their expected guest to arrive. At this hour of the night the street was dark and deserted with no traffic. Heart guessed it probably wasn't the smartest idea to answer questions about the illegitimate child your dead mistress was carrying in your home where your wife resided.

"So tell me again as number one and two in the house, why the hell aren't we resting in our beds this time of night?"

Heart tried to stifle the yawn that was rising out of her chest. Bryan was right, it was late and she was tired as hell. Something she'd been noticing more and more of lately. Over the last few weeks or so she'd be falling down by the time she stuck her key in the door. Then again she had been putting in more hours than normal on this godforsaken murder case too. She just needed a good night's sleep curled next to her husband and she'd be back to normal.

"Because it's considered poor etiquette to send a lowly detective to interview the head of the fucking state," she yawned out.

"If you ask me it should be in poor taste to be dicking the pretty young thing in your office when you're a married man old enough to be her father too, but I guess that ain't my business."

"You know how the rich and prestigious are Bryan, those people operate on a totally different wavelength than the rest of us."

Bryan raised a sarcastic eyebrow at her in response to her comment.

"What?" she questioned.

"You did not just sit here talking 'bout rich folks when you're one of them."

"Bullshit, my husband is rich, I just happen to be married to him."

They burst out in laughter until they saw the headlights of a dark sedan approaching. The car pulled up directly behind them and immediately killed its lights. Heart saw two dark figures cloaked in long dark coats and matching hats.

"A-yo, Bry, check out the get up this mofo and his lawyer got on."

"How do you know that's his lawyer and not security?" Bryan asked.

"He's a politician; his lawyer is way more valuable than security at getting his ass out of this current predicament."

Bryan took another look through the rearview mirror. "Seems your wrong, Captain," Bryan answered. "That's his chief of staff, Carl Meyers."

She nodded her head and both she and Bryan exited their car

simultaneously. They walked behind the car and stood in the space between the two parallel parked cars.

"Captain Searlington," the governor addressed her.

"Sir, are you sure you wouldn't be more comfortable at the station, or perhaps your office? I mean, it's late and this isn't the best area..."

He held up a hand. "No, this is fine."

"All right, sir; let's not waste your time or ours. Please excuse me if my questions appear to be a little abrasive, it's just that we need to get to the truth quickly in order to apprehend Ms.

Silverson's killer."

The governor nodded and leaned against the hood of the car behind him.

"Sir, how long were you sleeping with Ms. Silverson?"

"Since her junior year of college. The affair has been ongoing since then."

"Did you know that she was pregnant?"

The man stood, his shoulders sagging, seeming unable to bear the weight of his head. "Yes,

I did."

"If you knew about the pregnancy, what were you planning to do about it?"

"Do about it?" he asked. "I don't believe in abortion. Once Emily told me about the baby, there was no way I could ever ask her to terminate the pregnancy. I would never have asked her for an abortion."

Heart didn't give herself time to think about the inconsistencies of the man's morals. He couldn't abide by abortion, but he was certainly alright with lying and cheating behind his wife's back and disgracing his public office. She continued to ask the governor questions about his affair with the decedent.

"Who knew about the affair?" Heart asked.

"Just the two of us, my driver, and my personal assistant."

"What about your chief of staff?" Heart turned toward the man standing beside the governor. "Did you know about the affair, Mr. Meyers?"

The man was closer to Heart's age than the governor's. He was of average height and build. He looked to be of Jewish decent, dark curly hair, tanned skin, and dark eyes. But the truth was in the current light, Heart couldn't really make out much about his features.

"No, Captain. I didn't, not until the governor told me about this meeting with you."

Heart raised an eyebrow and returned her gaze to the ranking official in New York State.

"Why did you bring your chief of staff to this meeting, sir? I would have expected you to bring your lawyer to a meeting like this."

Myers interjected, "I am his lawyer, and that is exactly why he informed me of this meeting and asked that I accompany him."

I should have bet Smyth money. "Governor, do you think your wife suspected that you were having an affair with Ms. Silverson? Would she have sought to harm her if she did?" "Meagan?" he asked with surprise.

Heart warred with her need to roll her eyes. *You're stomping all over this woman's heart and public appearance and you think she couldn't muster up the courage to fix what she might have seen as a major thorn in her side. Yeah buddy, you're not delusional in the least.*

"Where were you the night Ms. Silverson was murdered?"

"I was at a charity event in Manhattan. There were two hundred guests there and plenty of media coverage to confirm my attendance."

"Don't worry sir," Bryan said. "We will verify everything you've told us."

"Will you be able to keep this sensitive information quiet?"

She looked up from her writing pad long enough to lock gazes with the man standing before her. He was a leader, he commanded, and instead of protecting those under his command he'd taken advantage. *Now you want favors?*

"Sir, there is an official record of your paternity of Silverson's child. There is no way I could bury that if I wanted to. My team is going to follow all of the leads we have, including the fact that you and your wife both now have a motive to have killed the decedent.

"I will tell you this is the last meeting we will have like this. Next time I interview you it will be official and it will be down at the precinct. You might want to do all you can to get out in front of this with respect to your office."

The man nodded his understanding. She wasn't hiding shit for this him.

"I didn't do this, detective. I loved her, and I would never have brought harm to her. My word still stands, whatever you need to further this investigation, I will make certain the mayor has it in order to give it to you."

She nodded and watched him carefully before she ended their meeting and motioned for Bryan to get back into the car.

"What now?" Bryan asked as he started the car.

Heart yawned again. "Now I'm going to take my ass home and go to sleep. I'll worry about whether this cheating son of a bitch killed his mistress tomorrow."

Bryan nodded and pulled their car into the street and headed for their precinct.

CHAPTER 13

*H*eart walked into the kitchen dragging ass after last night's incognito interview with the governor. She felt like she had the hangover from hell, body aching, head fuzzy, mouth feeling like something nasty was growing in it.

"Morning, baby." Kenneth's rich baritone attempted to cut through the murkiness in her head.

She put a hand to her pounding temple. "Please, no yelling."

Kenneth looked up from his coffee cup with question marks in his eyes. "Everything all right, Heart?"

She just groaned. Trying to think up words to say, "hurts too much," so she grunted out this sound that was a cross between a wounded animal and a dying engine. It wasn't the most appealing sound she'd ever made, but it was all she was working with this morning.

She headed for the counter in search for the coffee cup she knew Kenneth had waiting for her. Hell, if he was smart, he'd better have coffee waiting for her. On a usual day she wasn't really fit for public viewing until she infused her first cup of coffee. But today, today she was certain she was a danger to society with the all over dysfunction her body was indulging in at this moment.

She grabbed the cup and drank the coffee black with no chaser. Not really her usual style, but she couldn't afford to water down the dark brew. She needed high-octane gas this morning in its purest form if she was going to be worth shit today. And as much as she wanted to wallow in the funky way she felt, she had to get it together. She had too much fucking work to put in thanks to this new development in this Silverson murder case.

The fucking governor, she thought to herself. How a man of his intellect and stature could be so unbelievably stupid was beyond her. Power and promise at his fingertips, and now he was throwing it all away because he let himself be led around by his dick.

What the hell could this man have been thinking to actually believe he could get away with sleeping with his aide? Did he really think no one would ever find out? His career was fucked because he couldn't keep it in his pants. No matter whether the man was cleared of suspicion regarding the murder, he would most certainly lose his office for his soon to be revealed poor conduct and even more questionable judgment.

She took another large gulp of the coffee and her taste buds finally processed the acrid taste of the brew. Her face pinched in a disagreeable contortion and she lifted annoyed eyes to her husband sitting at the counter reading his paper.

"You do something different to the coffee?" she asked. She felt the bitter concoction hit the bottom of her stomach like a heavy stone. The pouch-like muscle in her abdomen rolled a little as the coffee splashed around a bit before it finally settled.

"No," he answered. "Just the same bean and water mix I use every day...that you claim to love."

"I don't know, it just tastes wrong," she answered.

She placed a soothing hand on her stomach and created a soft circular motion in an effort to quiet the little waves that were dancing on its lining. She looked at the coffee again and sniffed it this time trying to figure out why it wasn't agreeing with her.

"It even smells off."

Kenneth took the mug out her hand. He sniffed it, and then took a quick sip of it. After rolling the sample around his mouth and tongue, Kenneth swallowed and shrugged his shoulders.

"Tastes and smells fine to me," he confirmed as he placed the half-empty mug under her nose.

Holy hell.

The biting aroma of the coffee made her stomach lurch the wrong way and she felt its contents quickly climbing back toward her mouth.

"Oh God," she moaned and made a sharp about face turn toward the half bathroom in the hall. She made it just in time to spill the small amount of coffee that had climbed back out of her stomach and into her mouth. The hard tiles biting her knees, she paid homage to that toilet bowl as if it were her personal deity deserving of her worship, adoration, and praise.

She felt gentle fingers hold her hair back and knew that her husband was there with her.

Although grateful for his concern, she wasn't entirely certain she really wanted him to witness this vile biological act her body was forcing her to engage in.

When she was sure the last contraction of her stomach had passed and her torture had ended, she made an effort to pull herself up slowly from her kneeling position in front of the toilet.

"Hold on, baby, let me help you," Kenneth whispered and he pulled her up from the floor with strong hands fixed under her arms.

Heart went to the sink, washing her hands and face and rinsing the remnants of the foul taste in her mouth with warm water. She needed it all gone, didn't want anything left over that could send her back to the toilet for a repeat worship session.

She turned around to face Kenneth, still wiping the water drops from her freshly washed face. "Either you fucked up the coffee, or maybe I picked up some sort of stomach virus," she uttered.

"My coffee-making skills are as awesome as they've always been," Kenneth answered as assessing eyes walked over her.

"What?" she asked.

He tilted his head to the side, his gaze skating carefully over her. "Baby, you've been rundown lately. When was the last time you had a checkup?"

~

a
in't this about a bitch. She stared at the digital pregnancy test —because who had fucking time to be trying to decipher those goddamn pink lines on the non-digital type?—lying on the closed lid of the toilet in the small stall.

Pregnant.

That's what the damn stick said in bold, electronic, block letters.

Pregnancy was not something she'd ever given much thought to. *Obviously.* When she'd become captain, she'd gone on the pill to protect her from an unanticipated pregnancy. Too bad the damn things hadn't worked. *They didn't work, or you didn't take them like you were supposed to!* She couldn't even lie to herself. She'd forgotten to take those tiny little suckers more than she had forgotten her keys around the house.

She'd always thought that when and if she and Kenneth decided to have kids it would be something that took time. Didn't most couples have to plan, and try, and plan, and try some more? How the fuck had they managed to conceive off the absence of one missed pill? Weren't they supposed to build up some sort of immunity that lingered even when you missed a pill...or five?

That know-it-all conscience of hers was giggling its ass off right now. *You know damn well it doesn't work like that,* it said to her through bubbles of laughter. Wasn't shit like this supposed to take a few months at the very least for she and Kenneth to create another human being? *Are you really back to that shit, you're knocked up, deal with it.*

When she'd gone on the pill her doctor told her she shouldn't be surprised if it took up to a year to conceive after cessation of the pills. *Shit,* she hadn't stopped, just missed a couple and now, nearly four weeks after she'd remembered to stop missing her pills, here she stood knocked up, scared out of her mind, and leaning over the back of a toilet in a bathroom stall at work rechecking results that were glaringly obvious. She was fucking pregnant.

What the hell was she supposed to do now?

The scraping of the bathroom door opening shook her out of her daze. She snatched up that damn traitorous test, shoved it in her pocket and went to the sink to wash her hands. She was so grateful she'd thought to dispose of the box at the pharmacy before she'd driven in to work earlier in the morning.

On her way to work she'd thought about all the reasons she could be sick. Being sick was the only reason she could think of for not being able to stomach Kenneth's coffee. That man made amazing coffee. Sex and coffee, two things Kenneth did better than anyone else, two things she could never get enough of.

See that right there is why you're happy ass is in the predicament you're in now.

It was true, she couldn't deny she'd enjoyed every moment of getting this way. But even throwing up Kenneth's coffee hadn't made her suspect she was pregnant. She'd stopped at the chain pharmacy on Linden Boulevard and Seventy-Ninth Street to get something to settle her stomach. She'd been walking up and down the aisles looking for antacids when her eyes caught sight of all the conception planning products.

Let me hurry up and get the hell out of this fucking aisle, stomped across her brain loudly. Just as she was about to turn and find another aisle, three words danced across her forehead with hard ass metal taps on the heels.

Is it possible?

Since she couldn't give a definitive *no* as an answer, she grabbed up a digital test and paid for it at the front counter. The damn thing had practically burned a whole in her pocket the entire ten minutes it took her to arrive and park at work.

Now, she had her answer. The only problem was, now that she had it, she didn't really know what to do with it.

~

"*I*'d love to, but I don't think I'm going to be able to," Heart said gently. "I have to go to Mac's place tonight to cover for Big Willie. He asked me to take over tonight so he could have a night with Tee."

Kenneth took a measured breath. This was the third night this week he'd asked his wife to make time for him, and the third time he'd received no for an answer. Shit, at this rate, the only chance he'd have at seeing his woman was if she were arresting him.

"Heart, this is the third time this week you've covered for Willie, what the hell?"

Mac's Place was a community center Heart and her fellow officers spearheaded and maintained. It was on the outskirts of her precinct in Brooklyn. She mentored at-risk kids there when she wasn't working as top cop in her precinct.

Mac's Place was an amazing organization, and the regular kids that frequented the place had crawled their way into Kenneth's soul over the last two years. He loved those kids, would do anything he could for them. But damn, how much of his wife's time was he supposed to relinquish?

"Kenneth, he wanted a little mini-vacay. Why are you trippin' over this?"

"Because maybe I'd like to spend some time with my woman too," he growled through the phone. "Heart, last week you were swamped with meetings, and now this week you're filling in for Willie, I've barely seen you in almost two weeks," Kenneth answered.

He was pissed, a little more than pissed, but fighting with his wife about this wasn't going to fix the issue.

"Well then I'll meet you there. It's been a while since I hung out with the kids."

"Kenneth, I've got a lot of paperwork I need to do there, if you're there, you'll only distract me. Just go home; I'll get home as soon as I can."

Kenneth opened his mouth to answer, but Heart cut him off

quickly with a, "Something just came up at work and I gotta go," and before he realized it a dial tone sang in his ear.

He looked strangely at the phone, as if it held some secret to the mystery he seemed to be living in. When it didn't render any answers, he turned his chair to the side and let the city skyline fill his view.

"Hey, Kenneth."

Kenneth pulled his gaze from the large window behind his desk. He blinked a moment in order to focus on Alan.

"Kenneth, you all right?"

Kenneth didn't really know how to answer that. Something was definitely off, but he wasn't exactly certain what. He and his wife were out of sync. They weren't fighting, they weren't angry; still, something just didn't seem right.

"I'm all right, just thinking."

"About Heart?"

Kenneth smiled at Alan; he'd forgotten what it was like to have someone that knew him so well around all the time. He and John Tenetti had been close since childhood, but once his career as a recording artist took off, opportunities to just hang were far and few in between. The same went for Drew Marrack. Drew was a recording artist as well. He'd met him through John, and the three men had formed a solid friendship over the last few years.

Usually, Kenneth was alone to keep his own counsel. He knew his uncle David was always there for him if he needed, but usually he just worked his problems out alone.

"Yeah, she's been different lately," Kenneth answered.

"How so?"

"She just seems preoccupied, like something is messing with her focus."

"She is a police captain; she's working a major case right now that brings crazy scrutiny because of the players involved. Maybe it's just work stuff," Alan offered.

Kenneth shook his head. Alan's explanation was simple enough, but it just didn't seem to fit.

"I don't know, Alan. I just don't know that it's work. Heart is a natural at what she does. It's instinctual, like she was born to be a cop. She's never off her game when she's working."

"You guys haven't been fighting since the infamous club scene, have you?"

Kenneth laughed. Fighting, no, you had to actually spend more than five minutes together to be able to fight. This was different than fighting.

"No, things were fine once I realized she was working."

Alan leaned forward on Kenneth's desk his blue eyes squinting slightly. "You know, as soon as I got over the shock of seeing Heart up there, I knew she was working. Why didn't you? The moment you saw her, I could tell you were processing that entire scene as truth."

Alan wasn't wrong in his observation. He had reacted to the scene as if it were truth, because at that moment it had been truth. He'd never witnessed his wife during undercover work before. He'd never known that she was able to become another person when she was wearing the mask of her cover. But that's exactly what she'd done, and although he'd recognized her body, the person behind her eyes was someone he hadn't known.

"It felt real, and once it felt real, the rational part of my brain that should have known better, didn't. Once Bryan took me out to the SUV everything was fine. What can I say; I just don't like anyone touching my woman."

Kenneth shrugged his shoulders and pushed back into the comfort of his chair. "You were married before," Kenneth continued. "I know things ended badly between you and Alicia, but

I'm certain at some point you were irrationally jealous of some dude trying to poach on your

turf."

Kenneth watched Alan's blue eye dim with a saddened grey pallor and knew instantly he shouldn't have mentioned his friend's ex-wife.

"No, Kenneth," Alan spoke in a soft tone that seemed almost impossible for the heaviness of his adult voice. "I think that was the problem. I never felt so strongly for Alicia, that's why it was so easy for life to rip us apart."

"Alan, man..." Kenneth started, but was silenced by his friend's raised hand.

"Don't apologize. We both know that I should be able to tolerate the mention of Alicia's name. By now, it should be like water sliding down my back. But it's not, it still hurts."

Alan fell back into the chair and took a slow breath. Kenneth could see his friend trying to reign in all the unresolved emotions that had made him more than eager to move across the country to help Kenneth run his company. He carefully clicked each piece of his mask in place, but Kenneth could still see the fine fissures that marred it and screamed of Alan's untold pain.

"Kenneth, you and Heart have something real. Don't ever let anything come between that. If you want to spend time with your wife, then do it, even if she's making it difficult."

Kenneth nodded his head. Alan was right; there was nothing more important than what he shared with his wife. He would protect it at all costs.

❧

*B*ryan Smyth sat at the conference table at the seventy-fourth precinct scrutinizing every line of all three murder files sitting in front of him. This room had become his little sanctuary in the seventy-fourth precinct. More like hideout if he was honest. He chastised himself. He knew he was hiding, but truly, what else could you do when you made a complete mess of your personal life and everything at home reminded you of what could have been with your ex if you hadn't fucked it up.

It had been a few years now, and he still couldn't exactly say when things had gotten so bad with Jussy that they'd decided it was better to be apart. He just knew every day since, he'd ached some-thing awful and wished to God he hadn't agreed to their trail separation.

He shook his head; he'd royally fucked up by letting Jussy walk out of his life and now he was too much of a punk to face the empty damn hole in his heart that used to be filled with all the wonderful things Jussy brought to his life.

He shook his head and focused his thoughts back on this case. The medical examiner's report coupled with the lack of another victim solidified they weren't looking for the four corner's killer. He just couldn't quite figure out why someone was copying the serial killer's work. Was it to pay homage to the deranged fuck who'd been terrorizing three previous cities Agent Weaver had followed him to? Was it some sick kind of competition between the two? Or was there something else driving these three murders in Brooklyn?

He spread the photos of the three victims across the table willing them to show him what he was missing. Damia Grey, Blanca Fernando, and Emily Silverson each led separate lives, but managed to meet the same fate in the end: dead, mutilated, and alone.

"There's gotta be a connection between these three women. What the hell is it?" he asked the empty room.

Yeah, they all went to this same clinic, but none of them ever saw the same doctor twice. What was it about this place that linked all three women together? He knew it was there, just staring him in the face, so he went back over everything, hoping to connect the missing pieces.

When his eyes began to cross with fatigue, he stood up and stretched his legs to get his circulation going again. He walked out to the pantry and poured himself another bitter cup of coffee.

"God, could this stuff be more awful?" he asked no one as he took a swallow of the thick dark goop that passed for coffee in these parts.

"You've been working here how many years and you're still not used to the poison yet?" his captain asked.

Glad to be distracted from his thoughts he pointed toward the conference room and signaled his boss to follow. "Captain, you mind helping me out on something?" She nodded.

"I'm going to compile some data from these case files. I just need you to read off the names to me as we go through each of them. If I can get all the data in, maybe we can come up with a list we can cross-reference to get some understanding where this case is involved."

He and his captain worked in tandem as they picked apart the files. Digging for what, Bryan wasn't uncertain, but he knew something had to be in those files that they were missing. After setting up a blank spreadsheet on his laptop Bryan began plotting in the information MacKenzie supplied him with.

When they were done, Bryan sat back in his chair and adjusted the size of the spreadsheet so they could view all of the data on the screen. They checked carefully between the three women, trying to find a link between them and on the surface, there really wasn't one. Except for the free clinic they all patronized.

"Shit this is useless, we already know this," Bryan bellowed.

"Hold on there, number two. I don't think this is as hopeless as you believe. Look, the three women may not have seen the same medical staff at this place, but maybe…"

Bryan watched the captain pick up the files that were on the table. She went from one victim's file to the next in quick succession, scanning the pages in search of something.

"What'cha thinking, Captain?"

"What if the victims never saw the killer at the clinic? Maybe it wasn't someone that would have direct contact with the patients? What if it was someone who worked for the clinic, but not in a patient-care capacity?" MacKenzie asked.

"What, like a janitor?" Bryan queried.

"Possibly," she answered. "But I was thinking more along the lines of someone who might have access to patient files. Maybe it was someone like an office manager or medical billing coder that has to keep the books straight."

Bryan nodded his head and began to pick up the files himself. He scanned the folders until he found what he was looking for. "Shit, how did I miss this before?" he mumbled. "Captain Searlington, you might have cracked this case wide open."

She nodded nonchalantly. "I've been known to do that a time or two."

He laughed. "I'm sure that's part of the reason you're captain."

She shrugged. "That and the fact that I'm cute."

Bryan laughed loudly then. It never got old working with this brilliant woman who had spent so many years being his colleague, mentor, and friend.

"The same person signed off on the billing sheets for all three victims. That warrant we served to collect the vics' medical records, does it include electronic files too?" MacKenzie nodded her head.

"Then we need to go to the I.T. unit, they need to have a look see around the terminals at that clinic."

~

Heart stood outside of the examination room watching her detectives question the suspect through the one-way mirror. She turned her head slightly to the side to look at the governor standing next to her.

"Are you absolutely certain, Captain Searlington? Carl Myers is such a dedicated member of my staff. I mean, what reason would he have to kill Emily?"

"He overheard you and Emily discussing her pregnancy. He knew once the secret was out, you would be ruined, and more than likely ousted from office. He didn't want that. He believed wholeheartedly in you and your office. As your chief of staff he decided he had to get rid of Ms.

Silverson in order to save you," she answered.

"But why the other two women?"

"It was his attempt at hiding his crime. He'd read about the four corner's killer and thought if anyone cared enough to investigate the murders of two sex workers from Brooklyn, then they'd blame a known serial killer and not look at him. He wasn't banking on the clinic office manager telling us she sent the vics' files to him for some sort of government survey he claimed he was conducting."

"She's dead because of me, isn't she, Captain?"

Heart turned to him. She could see the sadness and guilt blanketing him like a murky cloud. "I can't answer that, sir. The only person that I can say with a reasonable amount of certainty is responsible for the death of that young woman and her unborn child is Myers," she answered him. "If you're asking me if Myers is the only one in this situation that should feel guilt and remorse? Well, only your conscience can answer that, sir."

Her eyes washed over the man at her side. Shoulders slumped, eyes red-rimmed, mouth sallow, he wore his guilt visibly. She could almost feel for him if he hadn't created the noose that was currently being fitted around his neck.

She took a breath and closed her eyes. *Please don't ever let me be stupid enough to wreck my perfectly happy life.*

If there was a god, and her grandmother had certainly taught her there was, then she hoped He heard her prayer. Because as far as she was concerned, nothing quite stung like knowing you fucked your own shit up.

~

*K*enneth pulled his luxury sedan into the parking lot behind Mac's Place. He looked around for his wife's car, but didn't see it.

Shit, I hope I didn't miss her.

He turned off the car and made his way around to the front entrance. Just as he made it in front of the building he saw Big Willie standing on the steps talking to the officer on duty. The officer turned and went back inside and Willie turned to face Kenneth as he walked up the steps.

"Fuck you staring at so hard, Searlington?" Big Willie bellowed.

Kenneth just shook his head. In all his years, Kenneth had never met anyone so blunt and loud as the retired police lieutenant. He was brash and confrontational, and although Kenneth would never admit it, he got a real kick out of the verbal sparring he and the older man engaged in every time they were in each other's presence.

"Not much," Kenneth answered making certain to put just enough disrespect in his voice when he did so.

"Fuck you, Searlington, don't think 'cause you're Porter's godson and MacKenzie's husband that I won't put a bullet in you."

Kenneth waved his hand. "We both know that shit is an empty threat, Willie." "Oh yeah, why's that?" Willie asked.

"Because we both know you fear my wife way too much to have her come for your ass for fucking with me."

Willie locked eyes with him for a beat longer before extending his hand to Kenneth. "Shit man, you ain't ever lied. You know your woman is crazy, right?" Big Willie asked laughing as he shook Kenneth's hand.

"Yeah," Kenneth answered. "But I kinda like her that way. What are you doing here, I thought you were on vacation?" Kenneth asked.

"Vacation, please," Willie waved a dismissive hand. "I wish. Nah, just round here with these little knuckleheads," Willie answered. "What brings you round here, young man?"

"I came to pick up my wife?"

"Here," Willie asked. "Mac ain't been here all week; she said she's behind in completing annual evaluations for her sergeants and lieutenants. I tell you, I do not miss that shit. Porter and

I used to be locked up for days on end in that damn precinct getting that damn paperwork done."

Kenneth let Willie's words sink in while he fought to keep the easy smile he had plastered across his lips.

"You musta' got your wires crossed, Searlington." Willie added.

"Must have." Kenneth nodded. "She probably told me the precinct and I just mixed it up." I'll head over there now."

Big Willie nodded his head, and shook Kenneth's hand again before walking back inside the community center.

Kenneth headed to his car with quick steps. He needed to be inside of it away from prying ears when he made the call he planned to. He slammed the door of the car with one hand as he put the phone to his ear, waiting for the call to connect.

"Smyth," Bryan answered.

"Hey Bryan, it's Kenneth."

He heard a familiar chuckle travel across the line. "Besides the fact that we have caller ID, you are aware your number is programmed into my cell. What's up man?"

"I was supposed to swing by the precinct to pick up Heart, but I got caught up at work. I've been trying to reach her, but she's not answering her phone. Is she still there?"

Kenneth hoped he was doing as good a job as he believed he was at keeping the anger out of his voice. If Bryan picked up on something in Kenneth's voice, he wouldn't tell him shit about Heart. Right now he needed candor, he needed to know for certain if his wife was lying to him about her whereabouts.

What, you need more proof than the fact that Big Willie was at the center instead of on vacation like your wife said?

Yeah, he needed more proof than that. She was his wife; she'd never given him reason to doubt his trust in her. He wouldn't willingly believe she'd violated his trust, not without substantial proof anyway.

His wife was smart, she was a cop, and she could think circles around most. If Kenneth wanted to know the truth of this crazy shit that was going on, he'd have to make certain she didn't have an explainable out.

"No. We had a really crazy day today, closed this murder case that's been all over the news for the last two months. After we finished interrogating the suspect, she said she was tired and needed to leave early. She didn't call?"

"No, she probably didn't want me to worry. If she'd called me I would have ended my work day and picked her up."

"She's been a little out of it lately, dragging really. I told her she pushes herself too much, all the hours she's been putting in are really starting to show," Bryan added.

"I tell her the same all the time, Bryan. She probably conked out as soon as she stepped in the house. I'm gonna head home now."

"All right," Bryan answered. "Tell her to call me let me know she's all right." "Will do, Bryan," he left the, *as soon as I find her,* in his head.

Do you need any more proof now? He ran a rough hand through his hair. No, he didn't need any further evidence to come to a very obvious conclusion. His wife was purposely avoiding him, and she was lying about her whereabouts to accomplish it. There was only one question he didn't have an answer for in this insane scenario. Why?

CHAPTER 14

*H*eart sat outside in her car and watched the lights of the television flicker in the dark living room through the curtain in the window.

She sat there trying to remember when things had gotten so bad between her and Kenneth that she actually dreaded coming home to him.

The day you took that pregnancy test, her conscience said.

She couldn't even deny it, it was fact. As soon as she'd learned she was pregnant, she'd instantly shut down. That was two weeks ago. And now she had to go inside after another night of lying to her husband and pretend everything was fine.

Kenneth wasn't stupid, he would figure out she was lying to him soon, if he hadn't already. She needed to just come clean with him. Just tell him that she was pregnant.

Then what? Will the two of you act like any other loving couple that finds out they're expecting? Will you smile, laugh, and cry? Will you celebrate? Will he be a proud expectant father, or...

She couldn't bring herself to think about the *or* anymore. She'd been running herself crazy with worrying about the possibility that Kenneth might not take the news of this pregnancy well.

In the two years they'd been married he'd never mentioned wanting kids. When she'd decided to go on the pill, he seemed to have no issues with it. They enjoyed a very full life together. The time they each dedicated to their respective careers barely allowed for a successful marriage, throwing kids into the pot might be the very thing that could break them.

She looked up to the window again, she needed to get inside before Kenneth started calling around and blew her cover all to hell.

She climbed the stairs, each taking more effort to scale than the last. She walked into the living room to greet her husband sitting on the long sofa.

"Hey, babe," she offered a brief kiss and sat down on the loveseat adjacent to the sofa, removing her shoes.

"How was Mac's place?" he asked casually.

"Fine," she answered.

"Just fine?" he responded.

"Yeah, it was fine. What's wrong with fine?" she asked him.

"Well," he began. "It's just that you usually leave that place doing cartwheels. The kids always give you an emotional high, even when they're getting on your nerves. But tonight it was just fine?"

The little hairs on the back of her neck began to stand up, sending a rippling chill down the center of her spine, pulling it into a rigid line. It was like her own internal warning system that was screaming, *danger, danger, danger*, in flashing red lights.

She stood up and walked to the kitchen, and wouldn't you know it, he followed her inside. She walked to the fridge to pull out some leftovers for herself. She placed the cold food on a plate and put it inside of the microwave.

"I really hope Willie appreciates you picking up the slack for him the way you have," he said.

"I'm sure he does, he knows how many hours I work. He used to be a cop. He knows better than most what a sacrifice it would be for me to takeover for him while he's away," she answered.

"Funny thing," he let a light chuckle escape the strange smile that was plastered on his lips.

"I don't really think Willie has any clue just how many hours you've been putting in at Mac's Place for this last while."

"And why is that?" she asked quietly as she turned to the microwave to stop the annoying beep signaling the end of the heating cycle.

She felt movement, felt him move across the kitchen, felt his front pressed against her back so lovingly it was painful to her. He leaned down to her cheek and pressed a cold kiss there, before he whispered in her ear.

"Because he didn't seem to have any clue what I was talking about when I saw him at Mac's Place. I was there looking to pick you up tonight. Imagine my surprise when Big Willie was standing in front of the building big as day."

He placed his hands on either side of her, laying them flat on the counter, effectively trapping her between his arms.

She was busted, there was no denying that. The only question now was did she come clean, or try to continue lying her way out it.

"And please don't insult me by telling me you were at the precinct, because I checked, and I know you weren't there either."

Well damn, she was right and truly fucked right about now, and so not in a good way.

❧

"Kenneth, I can explain," she uttered quietly.

"You can explain? You can *explain* why my wife has been lying to my face for the last two weeks? For damn sure you better explain, because neither one of us are leaving this room until I know exactly why my wife has been lying to me all this time."

He pushed away from her and walked back to the island in the center of the room. He ran brisk fingers through his hair then bound the messy loose strands with an elastic band.

"Where the fuck have you been? Why would you need to lie to me about where you've been spending all of this time, Heart?"

She turned to look at him. His beautiful cerulean eyes were filled with a dark anger that made them seem more navy than their usual crystal blue that she loved so much. He was angry, that was a given, but there was something more, something more prominent than the anger, there was...fear...worry.

God, how could she have been so selfish. He was worried; worried that something was wrong with them. It was all over his face, his features stiff and pulled tight, his posture just as rigid.

She shook her head; it hadn't even occurred to her that he would think her disappearing acts of late were an indication that something was broken with them.

I'm so stupid, no worse, I'm selfish.

She opened her mouth, but nothing came out of it.

"I swear to God, Heart, you'd better open your mouth and tell me something quickly. Make me understand this shit."

He was still, quiet. If anyone had stumbled upon them, his posture, the calm in his voice would belie the anger she could see building in his wild blue eyes. He was at his breaking point, pissed, and rightly so. Lord knows if the situation had been reversed she would have done worse than call him on his bullshit. She would have hurt someone, namely him.

She knew her husband too well, he wasn't happy. That cool veneer he was wearing was his greatest weapon in his business dealings. When people underestimated him in business, his pretty face lulled them into a false sense of security, leaving him more than enough room to exploit their weaknesses. She didn't have a prayer in all of God's heaven of walking out of this without giving him exactly what he wanted...the truth.

"Kenneth, this had nothing to do with you and everything to do with me," she revealed. "I've just been going through something unexpected, something I never figured on having to deal with at this point in my life."

She looked up and saw a flicker of concern mingled in with all of the anger swirling behind his eyes.

"Like?" he asked, sharp blue eyes still piercing her in the middle of her chest, demanding she keep her gaze locked on his.

"Kenneth…"

"Cut the bullshit, MacKenzie, and just tell me what that hell is wrong!"

Something in her cracked a little when he called her that. MacKenzie was her maiden name yes. It was the name she answered to at work. But from the moment Kenneth had discovered what her first name was—when she was lying in a hospital bed recovering from a bullet wound she'd taken to protect him and his family from his homicidal mother—if he wasn't attaching some term of endearment like baby or honey, he'd called her Heart.

Knowing he was the only one who called her that besides the family she was born to was like a little gift she carried with her all the time. Just thinking about it was one of the simple pleasures that often brought a smile to her face.

It stripped something in her to know that he'd chosen her maiden name, a name that held little meaning to her for so many years due to the estrangement she and her father shared at the time.

How much more will you allow this secret to damage his faith in you?

She could see it; the small chisel hammering away at what she'd once believed was an impenetrable thing. Heart was tearing them apart, and knowing she'd been the one driving this particular nail against the surface of their love made the brick currently sitting in her stomach press uncomfortably against her insides.

"I'm pregnant," she whispered.

~

f all the things he'd expected her to say, "I'm pregnant," wasn't one of them.

His mouth went dry. He it opened it twice before he pushed sound out of it. "Pregnant?" he asked more to himself than her, like he was confirming that his ears had in fact heard her whisper those words.

He relaxed against the island, some of the fight he'd been preparing to unleash on his wife's deception bled out of him.

"How long have you known?"

"Two weeks. I—"she started, but he sliced a quick hand through the air cutting off whatever she was about to say.

"Wait a minute, you've known about this for the last two weeks and you didn't feel the need to tell me? What, I don't warrant knowing that we've created a child together? I'm not on the 'in the know' list?"

She shook her head slowly. "It wasn't like that Kenneth, finding out just shocked me; I didn't know what to do."

He held his hands out in a questioning pose. "To do?" he asked. "What the hell do you mean by that? What the hell else was there to do, but tell your damn husband, unless?" Tension seeped back into his spine locking it in place, pulling him to his full height of six feet, three inches.

"Were you planning to terminate this baby before you even told me about it?"

She stumbled back against the counter with force, as if he'd hit her. He could tell she was surprised at his question. Her dark eyes filled with a watery shimmer, reflecting so much pain and confusion.

"I would never have done that, Kenneth. I never once considered terminating this pregnancy. I was just scared. I didn't know how to tell you."

From the first tear that slid down her tawny cheek, his anger fell away, and he moved to her, gathering her in his arms.

"Then, baby, help me understand. You're not some teenage girl, or a single mother. I'm here, I've always been here. Why would you think you needed to hide this from me?"

She pulled back just enough to look up into his eyes. He could still feel the tremors running through her. It made him physically ache to see her in such a state. The only other times he'd ever seen her like this was when she'd nearly died bleeding in his arms from a gunshot wound, and when her grandmother died.

He ran comforting hands up and down the lengths of her arms, using his touch to soothe her, keep her calm enough to express herself.

"We never talked about having kids," she spoke quietly. So quietly that even though he was holding her in his arms, he still had to strain to hear her. "I didn't know how you would feel about it. You never said kids were in the plan."

He was puzzled. No, he'd never explicitly said, "I want kids with you, Heart Searlington." But he loved her, and when you loved someone, you rejoiced at miracles like this, right? Why didn't she know that?

"Heart, I didn't really think I needed to say that. I love you, why wouldn't I love the idea of a baby with you?"

She shook her head. "Kenneth, I know you love me, I really do. But I also know that we knew each other for all of about six months before you rescued me from my demons, both physical and emotional, and married me. I know you didn't marry me to appease my dying grandmother, but even you have to admit that you probably wouldn't have proposed or even thought about marriage with me for a long time if Ida Mae hadn't been dying."

Was it wrong to want to shake a pregnant woman? He figured the answer to that question was yes, so he stepped away from her, putting enough distance between them that she was out of his reach.

"No, we're not going here," he responded. "This is the last time I'm going to say this, the very last time I ever want to have this conversation. I have told you before about telling me what

I want. I'm a grown man, and I know what I want, who I want. I married you because I wanted to. There is no other explanation other than that. From day one, I knew you were meant to be mine. I just didn't know how to make that happen because you fought me so damn hard. Did it ever occur to you that maybe, just maybe I wasn't trapped into this situation? Did it ever occur to you that maybe I used the unusual situations that were happening in your life at the time to get exactly where I wanted to be?"

She allowed questioning eyes to slide across his face. "Kenneth, you didn't manipulate me.

You didn't celebrate the craziness that I was drowning in just to get to me."

"No, Heart, I wasn't happy about all the pain you were in two years ago. But I'd be lying if I didn't say I recognized that your situation at the time opened a door that I'd been trying to beat down from the moment I met you. I have always wanted you, Heart. Loving you is not something that just happened accidently. From that first day in your office when you pulled your weapon on me to let me know who was in charge of Merridith's case there's only been one constant. My need and desire for you."

He saw the bubble of angst that was surrounding her deflate. He stepped in closer, bending down to touch his forehead to hers.

"Now can we cease with this bullshit?" he asked. "I don't know about you, but I'd much rather be celebrating this amazing news that we've created another life than arguing about why I married you. Nothing matters except this...I love you, Heart, and knowing you're carrying my child is the best surprise you could ever have blessed me with."

With those words she melted into him, almost as if she were trying to bury herself inside of him. Just like that, their connection was intact. He smiled, filled with a happy pressure that he was sure was going to explode all over him at any moment now. He was going to be a father.

He'd think about how scary that was later, right now; he would just enjoy holding the woman he loved.

～

*H*eart leaned back out of Kenneth's arms just enough to catch him grinning proud like he'd just done something spectacular. She didn't know whether to hug him, or slap that cocky ass grin off his face.

"We're having a baby!" Pride rose up out of his chest and beamed out through his eyes, ears, and every other orifice he had. His excitement was blinding her, making it difficult to look straight ahead into all that glaring happiness.

"Heart, are you okay?"

She closed her eyes and steadied her quaking insides. *He's happy, I was worried for nothing.*

"Heart?" she heard him ask again.

"I'm fine...I'm just...I can't believe it," she fumbled. "I just...I can't believe we did this."

He nodded in agreement. "I'm not so shocked," he mockingly cleared his throat and waggled his eyebrows. "...with the way you miss pills, and the fact that we work exceedingly well together in the bedroom department..."

She rolled her eyes and pushed him playfully in his arm. He pulled her quickly into his chest, burying thick fingers into her dark tresses and kissed her slowly. His lips gently met hers, skirting across her skin causing a zing of electric shock to sizzle across every inch of her body.

He had her so confused. She was scared out of her ever-loving mind one moment, the fear and shock of expectant motherhood speeding up her heart rate and blood pressure. The next, he kissed her, and she'd instantly forgotten about what she was so worried about two seconds ago. Damn she loved this man.

When he broke the kiss, the crystal blue of his eyes deepened to cornflower irises that sparkled with unshed tears.

"I never thought this would be possible for me, never thought I could love someone enough to have this. Thank you for walking into my life, and giving me this chance."

He blinked his eyes and a single tear traveled down each creamy cheek. She rose up on tiptoes and used each of her thumbs to smooth the moist tracks away. How this man could take her emotions from one extreme to the other, she hadn't quite figured out yet, but as long as he kept looking at her with those soulful blue eyes, she would gladly let him play her feelings like a master musician.

Standing here with him, basking in his happiness, the fear that had begun to sprout up inside her fizzled out like a wet candle. It was replaced by this strange sensation that niggled right beneath her rib cage somewhere inside her heart and added an extra beat.

She might be scared of the unknown and doing a little internal freak-out, but here, with Kenneth, the only thing she could feel was happiness. They were having a baby.

CHAPTER 15

*H*eart flopped down into her office chair. Damn, her day had just started and she already felt like she'd put in twelve hours. According to all the crap she read on the internet about pregnancy, fatigue was something that was par for the course during the early stages.

Dr. Sanderson was booked solid for the last week. Her first obstetric appointment would fall somewhere between what Heart calculated to be her seventh or eighth week of pregnancy. The first thing she wanted to know when she talked to the doctor was if there was something that could be done about this constant fatigue and dizziness.

She hadn't told Kenneth; she knew if she did, he'd flip out and try to make her start maternity leave today. Sometimes the dizziness was so bad she found it difficult to drive.

Yesterday she'd had to pull over on the shoulder of the Belt Parkway because her vision began to swim on her way to work.

After scaring the holy shit out of herself, she decided she would hitch a ride to and from work with her husband, telling him that she just wanted to spend extra time with him so they could share in the excitement of pending parenthood.

They'd decided to keep her pregnancy under wraps for now. They wanted to wait at least until the doctor told them everything was going fine before they shared this amazing news with the world around them.

Part of her wanted to hold on to this secret for just a bit longer. It was something else that only she and her husband shared, something else that spoke volumes of a quiet intimacy that joined them.

She heard a tap on her door and looked to find her second walking through her door. "We still doing our planned ride-around this morning?"

She nodded her head, not that she was particularly interested in sitting in a moving car for the better part of the morning, this baby did not seem to like the car much. Unfortunately, she still had a job to do. She nodded her head and started packing up her gear.

"Yeah, just give me a sec, I'll get my stuff together and we can leave. We can take your car."

Bryan looked at her strangely; she rarely let him drive her around. Captain or no, she just didn't like letting other people drive when she was in the car.

"You all right? I usually have to arm-wrestle you for the privilege. Everything okay?"

She nodded. "Yeah, I'm just tired; think I'm coming down with something," she answered. "Come on, let's go."

They passed the hours riding around, checking on their officers in the street. It wasn't something she did often; Bryan took over this duty mostly. But once in a few she would go out, make certain her people knew she hadn't forgotten about their welfare just because she moved up the professional ladder.

When they finished their rounds it was nearing lunchtime. "You up for hoagies from that bodega on Crossbay and Pitkin Aves?" she asked. Bryan nodded his head and turned their cruiser in the direction of the deli/minimarket. Her mouth watered as they neared the turn off of onto Crossbay. This was the best place to get a hero sandwich in Brooklyn, although technically the area was in Howard Beach

Queens, it was close enough for her to satisfy her craving. Bryan was about to get out and she stopped him.

"I know what you want. I'll take care of lunch if you take care of dessert," she pointed toward the new ice cream shop sitting on the opposite side of a shared parking lot entrance. "A quart of pistachio, please."

He raised a brow and opened his mouth to say something slick, she could tell, she'd known his ass too long to not see the insult on the tip of his tongue.

"Say something," she uttered through clenched teeth. "I dare you." She watched Bryan nod his head, lift his hands in surrender, and execute a perfect about face maneuver, heading in the direction of the ice cream shop.

She walked into the bodega and said hello to the attendant behind the register. She walked over to the deli section and put in their order. She moved to the back looking for drinks when she heard the chime of the bell over the door signaling someone walking in. She reached for the glass door of the refrigerator section when the distinct click of a gun rack sliding back and forth caught her attention.

She let the door to the fridge silently close and she stepped in between the isles, standing behind a rack of potato chips to keep herself concealed. She took a glance around to make certain there were no overhead mirrors that could reveal her hiding spot. As far as she saw, she was safe for now.

She quietly unbuttoned the snap of her holster. She pulled her phone from her back pocket and made sure the sound was set on silent. She tapped out a quick message to Bryan warning him not to come in and to call for backup.

After typing the message, she pulled her side arm from its resting place. She flashed her head around the corner to get a peek at what was going on at the register. Her eyes met with the middle-aged Latino man standing behind the counter. He gave his head a small and unnoticeable shake, warning her to go back to her hiding space. She moved her jacket to the side and watched as his eyes locked on to her badge with a small glimmer of relief.

She looked at him, hoping to God this man was telepathic, because she needed to know how many assailants were in the store. She waited a second, and saw the man run a shaky hand across his forehead. To anyone else, it would seem as if the man was simply wiping the nervous sweat from his brow. To her, she could see the man's slightly extended pointer finger. She lifted a single finger for confirmation and he gave an acknowledgement in a shallow nods.

She stole away to her hiding spot behind the chips and looked down at her phone. Bryan had received her text and was assembling a tactical team to handle the situation. The last line of his text asked her how she managed to find herself in scraps like this. She shook her head and rolled her eyes. *Fuck if I know.*

Help was on the way, she just needed to try to wait this out. They were in an enclosed space; bullets didn't always behave the way you wanted them to. If they both began firing, the two hostages could be harmed. She had to think this through. Unless she could get a clear shot at this guy, it was best to keep herself undetected for as long as possible.

She heard the gunman screaming at the two attendants in the front in Spanish. Damn was she ever glad she'd chosen to minor in the language in college.

"Dame el dinero! Todo ello, ahora!" the gunman screamed. He wanted their money. Hopefully the attendant would give the man what he wanted without argument.

"No jodas conmigo, sólo me lo da!"

Shit, the gunman was getting edgy, his voice was climbing. He was telling the attendant not to do anything stupid and just give him the money. She peeked out from her hiding spot and saw the panicked look on the deli attendant's face. Shit, this was not good.

She ducked down, and quietly stepped down the aisle. She chose the aisle that would put her behind the gunman, no need making him aware of her presence before she needed him to be.

She heard the gunman screaming more, shit was getting bad quickly. She texted Bryan, told him she had to go in, and to send help as soon as they arrived.

When she stepped out from her hiding space, the gunman was screaming and pointing the gun with angry stabbing motions toward the attendant. She grabbed a small metal can of something off of one of the shelves and threw it at the gunman, catching him on the side of his head. When he was distracted, she rushed him, knocking his gun out of his hand and taking him to the floor.

She jumped up while the man was still dazed and kicked his gun somewhere under the shelves where it was hidden from his reach. He jumped back up and took a wild swing her way, catching on her chin, making her bite into her lip. The taste of bitter iron began to fill her mouth, signaling the splitting of flesh.

When her assailant took another swing, she blocked it, and popped him in his mouth. It stunned him; she followed with another quick jab to his eye and he staggered back, trying to shield himself from her deft attack.

He prepared to charge at her, but she saw it coming and rolled with him, flipping him over and onto his back. She pushed to her feet and waited for his next move. He charged at her again like a bull, head down, because it had worked so well for him the first time. She shook her head and stepped to the side at the last minute allowing the would-be robber to crash into the ice cream freezer that was behind her.

Glass shattered all over, and he flopped to the floor. She turned him over on his stomach, jumped on his back, and affixed her metal cuffs to his wrists. She heard someone shout, "Police," and saw a swarm of her brother's in blue fill the store.

"I'm on the job," she said to the cops filling the small market. "Captain Heart Searlington, Seventy-Fourth Precinct."

These guys were cops, but they were from a different house out here in Queens. She was helped up into a standing position when she saw Bryan pushing through to get to her.

"What the fuck, MacKenzie?" he put a firm hand on her shoulder. "I leave you alone for five damn seconds and you end up in a hostage situation."

She started to say something smart when a blinding pain bent her over, folding her in half.

"Fuck!" was all she could say before her wind was cut short and another sharp pain tore through her lower abdomen.

"MacKenzie?" Bryan screamed.

"Bryan, something's wrong…please, get…a bus."

"Mac, what's wrong?"

She curled up to brace herself for another stabbing pain. "The baby…something's wrong with the baby!"

She heard a flurry of noise and felt herself being lifted from the floor; Bryan was carrying her and moving quickly through the store.

"I need a car now, she's pregnant and having abdominal pain!"

"Follow us," a strange voice yelled. She felt Bryan shove her into the back of a squad car and seconds later they were flying down the street with glaring sirens screaming in the air.

"Ma'am," she heard one of the uniformed officers say from the front of the car. "We're going to be there in just a second, you hang on."

Soon Heart felt the hard stop of the car. Bryan pulled her out of the car and gathered her back into his arms. They rushed her into the hospital. There was so much noise. She moved back and forth between cringing from the pain and jumping from the noise. And the light, it was so harsh and glaring. Her eyes slanted near shut and her entire body shuddered with fear. Fear for her unborn child, fear for herself, and fear of touch.

There was just too much of it, too much for her to try to filter through. Her breath hitched in hard pants trying to tell them about her condition, about this fear she'd spent most of her life battling. There was just too much for her mind to be able to focus. So she reached for the only thing that ever brought her comfort when fear was threatening to strangle her. She fought to take one solid breath, and with every fiber of strength she had to rise above the pain and panic she let a stark wail wrench from her throat and screamed one word, "Kenneth!"

~

*K*enneth was in the middle of a meeting when a cold chill bristled down each of his vertebrae. He heard a raging scream that pulled his head from one side of the conference room to the next. His heart rate inched up and his legs began to prepare to lift him out of the chair.

He felt a light tap on his shoulder and met the questioning gaze of his friend, Alan. He leaned in quietly and whispered to Alan," Something's not right, I have to go."

He stood and headed straight for the door. He was certain all the other sets of eyes in the room were glued to his back, but he didn't care. Something was wrong.

Kenneth walked passed his secretary as he headed toward the elevator bank. "Abby, I need to get home. Tell Alan I will call him later and fill him in. Cancel any meetings I have, I'll let you know tonight if I'm going to be back in tomorrow.

The ding of the opening doors captured his attention and he rushed inside hammering the ground floor button until the doors shut close. As soon as he stepped off the elevator his phone came to life. He saw Bryan's name scream across the wide electronic screen.

"What happened to my wife?" He blurted out into the air, turning for the executive parking garage.

"How did you—"

"Bryan, I don't have time for this, what's wrong with my wife?"

"She's having some kind of abdominal pain. We were in Queens getting lunch. Kenneth, she needs you here, I've never seen her like this. They had to sedate her because she kept fighting them."

"Oh God," he had to get to her. He turned the corner, his car in view, but he knew that wouldn't get him to Queens as quickly as he needed coming from Manhattan in late afternoon traffic. "Bryan, text me the info, I need to call my pilot."

Kenneth swiped his finger across his helicopter pilot's name. "Where are you? I need to get to Queens ASAP!"

"I'm inside the office. Tell me where we're going and I'll file a flight plan immediately. We can take off in as early as fifteen minutes."

"Do it," was all he said before he headed back to the elevator. When he stepped inside again, he whispered, "I'm coming, baby," and resumed stabbing the illuminated buttons.

~

Kenneth charged through the stark white halls of the labor and delivery unit looking for the nursing station. He was halfway there when he saw his wife's obstetrician walking through the halls.

"Dr. Sanderson, where is my wife, how is she?"

No more than five feet three inches and if she was more than a hundred pounds soaking wet

Kenneth would eat his own tie. He'd met her briefly when he'd accompanied Heart to an annual checkup last year. She had curly brown hair that swept her shoulders and flowed down to the middle of her back. Her face, usually lifted in a bright smile, wore a bleak expression, devoid of the laughter that usually followed her into a room.

"Mr. Searlington, let's step into the family room for a second." She led him to a small room at the front of the unit and she sat him down.

"They brought her in a storm of noise and chaos, it pushed her over the edge and the emergency room staff had to sedate her just to be able to examine and stabilize her. As soon as I was called, I told them about her haphephobia. She's been calm since then."

He noted everything she was saying, nodding in the appropriate places, and taking notice of the things she wasn't mentioning as well.

"The baby?" He felt the heaviness in his chest begin to build the weight making each breath noticeable and measured.

"Mr. Searlington, there is a serious problem with the baby. Before Heart collapsed she was in some sort of a hostage situation in a robbery gone wrong. From what witnesses say, she was able to apprehend the assailant, but she did get into a physical altercation in order to do so."

"Did that cause the problem with the baby?" he asked trying to make sense of what she was attempting to tell him.

"No, ironically, that altercation is probably the thing that saved her life. Heart has an ectopic pregnancy. Do you know what that is?"

He racked his mind, trying to make sense of her words. "Is that when the baby develops outside the womb?"

She nodded, sadness marring her soft features. "The baby implanted itself in her fallopian tube instead of her uterus."

"What does that mean exactly?"

"It means that if I don't intervene, the baby will continue to grow. The fallopian tubes are not meant to host a healthy pregnancy. Eventually the tube will burst, and Heart will likely die as a result of it. We need to surgically end the pregnancy in order to save Heart."

He couldn't pinpoint the moment the tears started falling, he only knew he felt a soft comforting hand at his shoulder. He controlled his breathing; he couldn't allow himself to shatter into tiny pieces right now. He had to get to his wife.

"Does she know?"

The doctor nodded. "I told her, but she's not ready to hear it. She accused me of trying to take her baby. She won't give us consent to perform the surgery."

Kenneth stood up and walked to the small window in the room. "Dr. Sanderson, I need to talk to my wife."

The doctor escorted him out of the room and walked him to a trauma room door. Kenneth slowly opened the door and found Bryan sitting protectively next to his wife's bed. If it couldn't be Kenneth, or blood, Kenneth was relieved to see someone there protecting his wife and baby.

"Kenneth, man…"

Kenneth allowed his weary shoulders to droop a little more in the presence of his wife's work partner, and more importantly, their friend. Bryan was someone else that loved her, and right now the two of them were going to need as many people like Bryan as they could get surrounding them—people that loved them as hard as they could.

The two burly men fell into each other's arms; both needed the other's strength, both trying to comfort the other. They'd been here before, watching this woman that they both loved fight for her life as a result of trying to protect others.

Kenneth was the first to step out of the embrace. "I need to call True. It's not good, man."

Kenneth pulled his phone from his pocket and dialed his wife's best friend, her cousin True. He waited for the call to connect and heard the audible gush of air that rushed out of his lungs in relief.

"Speak," she said. If the situation wasn't so serious, if it had been any other day, he'd joke with True about her bluntness. But today wasn't that kind of day. Today he needed Dr. True Amare, not his intellectual sparring partner that he usually went round for round with.

"True, I'm in the hospital with your cousin and we've got a serious problem."

"What happened?"

"Heart has an ectopic pregnancy."

"Pregnancy? How far is she?"

"Almost eight weeks, we just discovered the pregnancy. The doctor wants to take the baby, but Heart won't consent."

"Damn that woman," True mumbled through the line. "Listen, Kenneth. She has no choice, if her tube bursts, she will die."

"True, she's capable of making her own decisions, it's not like I can stop her."

"Fuck that bullshit, Kenneth. That's my fucking cousin and your wife. You know damn well she's not thinking clearly. If she were, she'd let the medical team do what needs to be done."

There was that straightforwardness that True was so famous for. "True, this isn't a tumor we're talking about, some benign thing with no significance. This is our fucking child."

"This is her fucking life," True countered. "Kenneth, I know this is

164

difficult, and I don't mean to minimize the situation you're in, but you can't let her do this. It's suicide."

Kenneth felt Bryan tap him on his shoulder. When he turned around, he could see dark lashes lifting in an unhurried flutter.

"Kenneth?" her meek voice filled the room.

He slid into the chair at her bedside and enclosed his hand around hers. "I'm here, baby."

She pulled herself up into a sitting position and clambered on to him. He could feel the shivers of fear that riddled her body.

"They want to take the baby...please don't let them!" Her excited words wrapped around his heart like an angry fist. She was so scared, more than he'd ever witnessed in their history together.

Heart Searlington was never a helpless person. Even at the depths of her fear she always pushed through whatever the situation was and dealt with it. That was who she was, that was part of the reason she was such a great cop. But here in his arms, fear was winning.

He pried her arms from around his neck and leaned back just enough to fasten blue eyes on to brown. He smoothed his fingers over her hair and repeated the motion until he saw some of her anxiety fall away. She laid down, losing some of the stiffness the panic pushed into her limbs. He continued to stroke the skin of her hand to aid her relaxation. Perhaps if he could get her to calm down she would see reason.

Exactly how are you going to get her to see reason when you can't understand this yourself?

It was true, he didn't get this. They were happy; they'd created this new life. Now this new life that they both adored might actually cost him the woman he loved.

"Baby, this is a very serious situation. Your body can't carry the baby. You are in danger of dying. Heart, we have to think very carefully about the decisions we make right now."

"Kenneth, don't let them—"

He placed a single finger across her lips, quieting her. "Baby, we have to do what's best here. You could die." Just saying those words made his stomach twist in pain. "We have to keep you healthy."

Kenneth heard the door open behind him and watched as Dr. Sanderson walked in. Her face was void and still, a stark contrast from her normal demeanor. She sat down on the opposite side of the bed from Kenneth and looked down at Heart.

"Heart, you've been a patient of mine for a very long time. So you know me, you know if there were any other way, I'd move heaven and Earth to have you and the baby come out of this healthy. I cannot advise you to attempt to maintain this pregnancy. I've just gotten back more of your test results, including the scans we ran. We have to get you into surgery. The only reason you're not doubled over in pain is because we have you on morphine. This is going to end badly if you don't have this surgery."

"No," Heart said as she sat up in the bed. She swung her legs to the side attempting to get out of the bed.

Her feet were an inch away from the floor before Kenneth stood in front of her, preventing her from standing up.

"What the hell are you doing?"

She tried to maneuver around him, but again he stopped her. "I'm not going to let her kill our baby," she cried out. She aimed for the I.V. in her hand, but the doctor grabbed it before she could rip the taped catheter out.

"Heart, if you don't calm down, I'm going to sedate you again."

"I'm not letting you kill my baby!"

Kenneth stood in front of her and wrapped his arms around her, pressing her face into his chest, cradling her like a scared child.

"Sshh, baby. It's okay. I'm gonna take care of everything."

"Promise me, you won't let her do it...please, Kenneth."

"I promise to take care of everything." He continued to stroke her as the doctor pressed buttons on the I.V. Soon he felt Heart's muscles go slack. The morphine had done its job. He gently placed his wife back in the bed, and kissed her smooth brow before turning to the doctor.

"Give me the papers." He loved this child, but he couldn't lose his wife. His only prayer was that in saving her, he hadn't lost her anyway.

CHAPTER 16

THREE MONTHS LATER...

Heart looked out the kitchen window into the navy-purplish color of the early morning sky.

She was up early, earlier than she really needed to be. She'd rolled out of bed, leaving her sleeping husband still buried beneath the covers.

She'd quietly tip-toed out of the room, showered and dressed, and gone downstairs to gather her things before she left the house. She checked her weapon, secured it in her hip holster and then rechecked it again before heading out.

Today was her first day back to work since...in three months. Her body was healed, her doctor had cleared her to return to duty. The only thing left to do was get out there and get back on the job. She needed to get back out there, had to. Sitting in this fucking house being smothered by her well-meaning friends and family was going to kill her if she didn't break free soon.

They loved her, she knew they did, but if someone else told her they knew how she felt, how hurt she was after losing a baby, if one more person said that ignorant shit to her…

She took a break, pulled her shit together. She couldn't lose it. If she couldn't keep it together she'd lose yet another thing she loved and that might just break her. Not that she was all that far from crumbling now. Every time she thought about waking up in that hospital bed, being told that her husband had signed papers giving them permission to kill her baby—she just couldn't go there again. It wasn't healthy for her, but work, work would make her forget.

She made the quick trip down the Belt Parkway and parked in her designated spot behind the precinct. She sat quietly in the car trying to get herself ready to walk into that building. It really shouldn't be this hard; with the exception of Bryan, no one in the precinct knew what happened to her.

Internal Affairs had interviewed her after they'd been informed she was rushed from the scene to a hospital. She assured them that her injury wasn't due to the attack, but because of a health problem she'd not been aware of before that situation.

A health problem, from that moment forward, that's all anyone would ever remember her baby as—something that need to die so she might live.

She shook it off, and pulled herself out of her car. She grabbed her bag and headed through the doors. She just needed to get inside, once she was there, everything would be fine, normal even.

The first person to notice her when she opened the door was the desk sergeant. He stood up and lifted a stiff, pointed hand to his temple in salute of her. "Attention, Captain on the premises."

The usual buzzing that filled the squad room ceased and her officers all mirrored the desk sergeant's stance. She was so proud of the sight of her officers, any commander would be. But knowing she wasn't worthy of the honor they were giving made the coffee she'd ingested during her ride to work want to climb back up her throat.

They thought they were saluting a woman who had been injured in the line of the duty. If only they knew that there wasn't a thing worthy of honor in her. The one thing she'd been born to do, her traitorous body had failed at it. Too ashamed to enlighten them of her personal failing, she simply nodded and gave them permission to return to normal duties.

She made quick work of getting inside her office. Standing out there, knowing what all of them thought, it was just too much for her to handle. Quiet, that's what she needed, and her office would give her the solitude she needed to set her emotions in order, to distract her from the hole that was trying to suck the life out of her from the inside.

Her cell phone rang as she sat down in her chair. It was her husband's ringtone; he was probably just waking up, realizing she'd left without saying a word. She contemplated letting the call go to voicemail, but with the way Kenneth had been watching her lately, like she was going to flee or worse yet, break apart if he didn't monitor her every second of every day, the wiser action would be to answer him.

"Hey," she stated simply.

"Hey yourself," he answered. "You didn't wake me this morning."

"No, I've been gone for three months, I just wanted to get in and get straight to work. I have no idea what's waiting for me now that I'm back."

"I don't think taking five minutes to say goodbye to your husband would have made all that much of difference in your workload."

She rolled her eyes, this was getting really old. Ever since she'd come home from the hospital he'd been all over her night and day. He monitored her mood swings more than she did and the only thing it made her want to do was get away from him as quickly as she could.

"Kenneth, I have work to do," she replied. "I can't really get into this now. I'll see you tonight." She ended the call before he could respond and made herself comfortable behind her desk.

She looked down and saw that the desk was exactly as she'd left it. Her laptop sat in the center. Her desk phone was off-center to the right. Her pen was positioned on top of the yellow legal pad sitting between the laptop and phone. It was like a shrine to the day that she'd like to least remember.

The brief tapping noise pulled her attention to the door where she saw the smiling face of her lieutenant. His questioning eyes assessed her, asking her if she was okay. She nodded in response.

"So, Lieutenant Smyth, tell me what's been going on in my absence."

"Pretty much the same thing as always," he answered. "There's nothing that you can't catch up on in a day or so."

"What about your team?"

"They're working on a murder case that just came through, but other than that, everything is normal."

Yeah, normal, that was exactly what she needed. To find normal again, she needed to be normal again. Truth was she really had to wonder if she'd ever had it.

~

$\mathcal{K}$enneth sat typing out reports in his office until the buzzing of his intercom interrupted his progress.

"Yes, Abby."

"Sir, Captain Porter is here to see you."

Kenneth glanced at his open calendar quickly to see if he'd forgotten a scheduled meeting, but just as he'd thought, the slot for the day was empty. He stood up and went to the door to greet his godfather and met the smiling face of the man who'd help raise him.

"Uncle David, what are you doing here?"

"I gotta have a reason to come visit my only godson?"

Kenneth folded his arms and laughed a little. "Pretty much, we both know how much you hate the city."

"I do."

They moved inside and Kenneth retrieved two bottles of water from the minibar and handed one to his godfather before sitting next to him at the conference table.

"Water? Damn, I mean, it's not like I raised you or anything. Can't you spare some of the good stuff you use to schmooze those big wigs that come in here?"

Kenneth shook his head. "Not really, those big wigs pay me millions of dollars at a time, you mostly pay me no mind, so no, you can't have any of my expensive liquor. Besides, we both know Aunty Pam would kill me."

The elder man waved a dismissive hand through the air. "Ain't nobody scared of Pam."

"I am," Kenneth said. "And if you were smart, you would be too."

David Porter laughed along with Kenneth. For all of his bluster, anyone who truly knew David Porter, understood that his wife Pam was his heart. She was nurturing and loving, but that didn't mean she wouldn't tan your hide if you crossed her the wrong way. Kenneth had spent many years witnessing the dynamic between the two. His godparents had been his only positive model of marital bliss as a child. They'd been the ones to teach him about love and family. A lesson he still carried with him today.

"Speaking of crazy wives…how's yours?"

The smile leaked slowly off of Kenneth's face. It wasn't that he couldn't answer that question. It was more like he wasn't certain if he should.

"Today was her first day back at work," Kenneth answered instead.

"I know," Porter replied.

Kenneth gave Porter a sidelong glance, tilting his head as his mind made sweeping calculations.

"She told you?" Porter shook his head.

"I know I didn't tell you. So how did you know?"

Porter took a long swallow from the water bottle Kenneth had given him before he returned his gaze to Kenneth. "I don't need to ask her to know what she's doing, I'm her former commanding officer, I always know what she's doing."

"That sounds kind of stalkerish."

Porter shrugged his shoulders in a casual way. "So you say. I call it just taking care of my people. How's she really doing? Your aunt and I haven't seen much of the two of you over the last three months."

It was true, once Heart had been released from the hospital, she'd declined visitors altogether. Splintered by the pain of loss, she chose instead to stay hidden in the bedroom unable and unwilling to let anyone in, including him.

He was ashamed to admit it, but in the three months since the loss of their child there had been this growing chasm of distance between them. It made him uneasy. Everything within him wanted to sit her down and force her to face the unspoken issues between them. But Heart didn't deal well with emotional confrontation.

If you asked the woman to literally dodge bullets, she'd slap that all powerful "S" on her chest and do it without flinching. Try asking her to confront her emotions, break through the emotional waves that were crashing down over her head threatening to drown her...nope, not a chance.

She'd always buried her head in the sand where her feelings were concerned, but Kenneth had always been able to reach her, help her see that her secrets, her repression only made things worse.

"She's dealing as best she can. I don't think she's over losing our baby, but she's functional enough to do her job."

"I'm not worried about her job, boy, I'm worried about her. Is she all right; are the two of you all right?"

Kenneth stood up and walked to the window, needing to put a little distance between he and his godfather. The man had a habit of seeing past the bullshit walls people put up to hide their shit, and seeing right through to the gooey core.

"I'm worried. I don't know if she and I will ever get back what we had. That day, it just made it harder to connect. She's still healing, she's still processing all of this, it's just not been easy for her to put this entire situation to bed."

Kenneth felt Porter's thick hand on his shoulder. It was something the man had always done, his way of saying, "I'm here if you need me." Kenneth nodded; Porter's support had seen him through considerable challenges in his life. He could only hope it would be enough to see him through the other side of this current transition.

"However bad it is right now, don't lose that connection son. Fight for it, even if you have to fight her. You can get through anything if you have that connection, the thing that bound you together in the first place. Lose that, and there's no hope of ever making it work again."

Porter turned around and headed for the door, he stopped briefly and turned halfway toward Kenneth again.

"The governor is honoring several members of the varying law enforcement agencies at some sort of gala next month. I'm being honored, and so is your wife. I'm sure she hasn't told you; even though I know for a fact she's been notified already. Don't let her miss this, and if you need to light a fire under her, tell her Pam promises to tan her backside if she isn't there."

Kenneth laughed. His godfather was correct, Heart hadn't told him shit about this event, and he was very certain his godmother had given Porter those exact words to say. Maybe a quick swatting from Aunt Pam would help his wife get it together. Lord knew nothing he tried to date had managed to work.

He walked David Porter out of the office and to the elevator with a promise that he and Heart would be all right. *If only I knew that were true.*

He really had no clue how they were going to pull themselves back from the growing hole between them. It just felt bigger and deeper every day.

He flopped back into his chair and took a long breath, trying to beat back the grief that he often buried beneath work, and contracts, and concern for his wife.

It hurt. There was no other way to describe what their loss felt like. It was big, and overwhelming and there were days he thought he'd drown from the overwhelming weight he shouldered every day, but he couldn't really deal with that. There was no time to worry about his pain and grief, because Heart needed him.

Heart needed him, even though she pushed him away and kept him at arm's length. She needed him to keep shit together for the both of them. And he did, he kept everything on track. But more and more lately he worried that the raw emotions he was stomping down on would explode and incinerate everything they held dear in to infinite little pieces.

Because that's what happened when you were pretending everything was fine, soon, shit exploded.

CHAPTER 17

"*M*acKenzie, aren't you going to call it a night?"

If she had any damn sense she would, but she'd never been accused of being the brightest bulb in the room.

"I'm just trying to catch up with all the work I missed these last three months."

"MacKenzie," Bryan said. "You've been back two weeks, and you've spent every one of those two weeks bolted to that damn chair, or running around this precinct like some sort of efficiency officer."

"Bryan, I'm the captain, that's kinda sort of my job."

"MacKenzie, go home."

"I'm working, Bryan." She threw down the file in her hand and rubbed tired eyes that were blurring from the strain of overuse.

"Working or hiding? Which one?"

She rubbed the back of her neck, trying to loosen the tension this conversation was beginning to cause.

"You know you haven't said one word about it."

"Am I supposed to know what you're talking about, Smyth?"

Bryan gave her a pointed gaze, and then stepped inside of her office, closing the door with a soft click. His usual relaxed features were morphed into tight lines and pinched brows. Whatever he was about to say didn't bode well for the peace of mind she was working hard at securing.

"MacKenzie," he said softly once he'd sat in front of her. When she didn't lift her gaze to him, he called her again. "Look at me, this is important."

She stopped what she was doing and complied with his request. Behind thick dark lashes she saw concern. He'd shown that concern when they were cadets struggling in the academy together, and again whenever they walked into something dangerous when they were partners.

He'd shown it when she'd been shot two years ago, and certainly when she'd doubled over in pain three months ago. His concern had always cloaked her like a warm garment, protecting her from the cold, but this time was different. This time, the cold was just too bitter. It ate away at all of her protective layers seeping inside, biting at the sensitive pieces of her soul.

"What is it, Bryan?"

"Why haven't you mentioned it?"

"I assume by it you're referring to the fact that I had my child ripped from my body in a cruel twist of fate. Is that the it you're speaking of?" She slapped the pen she was holding in her hand down and flexed her hands in and out of tight fists.

"Bryan, my baby is gone. I know that, I accept that. I'm sorry if I'm not living up to everyone's expectation of normal. I'm sorry if I'm not falling apart in front of all of you. I was devastated, but I can't wallow in that. Talking about it is the last thing I want to do, I don't want to remember any of it. Hell, I'd do anything to forget. But every day I wake up, every single time I open my eyes it is the first thought I have.

"Every minute of every day the fact that my baby died plagues me, no amount of talking about it is going to change that. No amount of reliving it is going to make me feel better about that shitty fact. Nothing will help, so why do you think I should talk about it, why would I want to?"

He stood up and walked behind her desk and kneeled next to her.

"No one expects you to forget. We just don't want it to drown you. Don't push us away." *Too late*, she thought. She was already drowning.

∾

$\mathcal{K}$enneth looked down at his watch as he climbed out of the car. He was still making good time to execute his plans for the night. He walked through the door leaving his briefcase on the floor and running upstairs to get out his work clothes and into something comfortable.

He donned an A-line t-shirt, and dark sweats tied loosely around his hips before setting bare feet on the stairs and making his way to the kitchen. He looked at the digital clock on the stove he estimated he had another ninety minutes or so before his wife made it home.

He pulled the needed ingredients from the fridge and started working on their dinner. His godfather's words filled his thoughts again.

However bad it is right now, don't lose that connection son. Fight for it, even if you have to fight her. You can get through anything if you have that connection, the thing that bound you together in the first place. Lose that, and there's no hope of ever making it work again.

"You might be a pain in the ass sometimes, Uncle David," he said to no one. "But on this you ain't wrong."

Kenneth felt the gap widening. Slowly, every day, his wife retreated inside herself. It wasn't anything major, there had been no huge changes in routine, but in Kenneth's estimation, all of the little small things added to the fact that he and his wife weren't connecting as a couple.

They ate together, slept together—and for the first time in their marriage that wasn't a euphemism for sex, sleeping was all that was going on in that bed. They spoke; conversations were boiled down to polite exchanges of need-to-know information, but the truth was, they weren't sharing much of anything—actually, she wasn't sharing anything at all.

He'd never had to work so hard to make inroads with her, not even at the beginning. Hell, in the beginning, she'd pulled a gun on him twice and he still felt they connected more, better, deeper, than the sickeningly civil shit that they were dishing out now.

Tonight he was going to take steps to end that. To get back to where they were before life tried to break them.

He felt the familiar tightness in chest that crept up inside of him every time he thought of their lost child. He'd only known about their baby for a few weeks, but that was more than enough time for him to become completely enamored with the tiny being that rested inside of his wife.

From that first moment she'd uttered those words to him, he lost the other half of his heart to this person that wasn't even bigger than the top of a nail pin.

His eyes started burning with the memory of their loss. The child he would never know, the baby who was taken from them. He put down the spoon he was stirring the simmering pot with and turned the water on in the sink. He cleaned his hands, and then ran cool drops over his face. Tonight would not be about their sorrow, rather their reemergence from the flames.

Dinner was almost ready, Heart would be home soon. He pulled a bottle of wine from their wine fridge in the pantry and opened it up to let it breathe. The glow of headlights in the backyard brought a smile to his face, she was home, and he was going to set things right.

He poured a healthy glass of wine for both of them and grabbed one and headed for the door. When the door opened, he was standing there, glass in hand, with a nervous smile.

She looked around the room, inquisitive eyes processing the scene. "Everything all right?" she asked.

"It will be," he whispered before closing the space between them and lowering tentative lips to a mouth he knew so completely. That first kiss was soft and slow, asking permission. When he met no resistance he deepened the kiss, pressing determined lips to hers, licking the fullness of them, savoring the brilliant taste he'd spent so long aching for.

He felt life awaken just below the waist of his sweats. His dick thickened and twitched just enough to let him know that if he really wanted to dine on something other than his wife's body, he'd need to stop now, or resign himself to cold leftovers.

He gentled the kiss, leaving soft pecks on her lips before he stepped back and gifted her with a smile.

"Hi," he said.

"Hi yourself," she answered with a weak lift of the corners of her mouth. "It seems like you've got plans."

"Nothing more than spending some time with my wife," he bent down and gave her another quick peck. "And enjoying this amazing bottle of red wine I just opened up. Care for a taste?" He handed her the wine glass and watched her take a sip.

"You're right, that really is good wine. Why don't you finish it up?"

"You don't want any?"

She shook her head, "No, I had a really long day and my head is killing me. I think I'm just going to shower and get right to bed."

He could almost hear the audible pop in his bubble of expectations.

"Is it that you don't feel well, or is it that you just don't want to spend time with me?"

He watched her, eyes slightly widened in surprise. She was either shocked that he'd voiced the question, or shocked he'd been able to come to that conclusion at all.

"Kenneth," she said barely meeting his eyes. "I'm just tired, that's all."

He stepped back and gave her room to maneuver around him. She quietly disappeared up the steps leaving him to process the scene around him.

"And to think this night started out with so much promise," he grumbled.

He re-corked the wine and packed up their uneaten dinner in plastic containers. He cleaned up the used pots, and grabbed the two mostly full wine glasses off of the counter. His first thought was to empty them into the sink, but decided good wine shouldn't go to waste just because his night went to shit and emptied them both in a few monster swallows.

Dishes in the dishwasher, countertops wiped clean, floor swept, Kenneth turned the lights off with a soft click and headed upstairs. He ambled into their bedroom and sat down. Not quite certain why he was here—in the bedroom, in the marriage—not certain if his presence in either was welcomed any longer.

He watched Heart amble out of their master bath in a cotton sleep shirt, feet covered in thick socks, hair wrapped around her head and tied with a huge floral silk scarf. This was her, "I'm not trying to be bothered with you," look that he'd only seen sparingly throughout the course of their two-year marriage. Except these last three months, she'd come to bed dressed exactly like that every night.

"I can't do this anymore," he said, his words stopping her forward motion causing a heavy silence to fill the room.

"You can't do what?" she asked.

"This," he said waving an animated hand back and forth between them. "I can't just sit by and watch you pull away from me anymore. It hurts, Heart, I mean, it physically hurts because I know where this is going. It's a slow death, you're ending us."

"Kenneth, this is a little melodramatic, don't you think? Just because I don't feel up to having sex with you, I'm instantly sabotaging our relationship?"

He shook his head. "It has nothing to do with the fact that you won't make love with me.

This has everything to do with the fact that you are closing me out of your heart."

"Kenneth, I don't think it's that serious."

He jumped up from the bed and met her where she was standing.

"Really?" he asked. "Not that bad? When was the last time we made love, Heart?"

"Kenneth, don't act like I just decided to stop having sex. I had surgery, I lost my baby."

Kenneth let that shit wash over him while swallowing the bile that was rising with his temper.

"Yes, you had surgery, yes, you were cleared to resume your regular activities of daily living six weeks later, and yes, you lost *our* baby, Heart. Not yours, not just yours, *ours*. You've been walking around this house in your own little world locking everyone out, including me, *especially* me. I lost a baby too. When does my fucking loss register? When does my pain matter?"

"Whatever, Kenneth, I'm not in the mood for your shit. You're mad 'cause you can't get your dick wet, well, that's on you. Either rub that shit out, or let your motherfucking rocks turn blue for all I care, but I'm not in the mood."

"This has shit to do with me getting off and you know it. You're my wife, we lost a baby—"

"No!" The raw sound filled the room making the inside of his ears throb. "No, you didn't lose shit. I lost—"

She stopped herself. He could see the tremble vibrating the very skin on her body. He'd known this is what it would come to, had always not so secretly understood that this was where all the rage came from.

"Say it," he growled through clenched jaws. "Say it."

Her chest heaved with the pent up rage she'd been carrying, subduing all this time. She'd hidden it, clamped it down, suppressed it until it became a living breathing thing, and now she was poised to let the truth slip from her lips for the first time in more than three months.

"I lost a baby, and you...killed it."

He'd known. The words shouldn't have been a surprise. He'd felt the undercurrents of her resentment from the moment her brown eyes fluttered open in post-op. He'd known then that this truth would eventually need to be spoken, but he somehow thought they would have worked through it together.

Instead, he stood there wobbly from the blow. What else did you call it when your wife called you the murderer of your unborn child?

The pain sawed through him with jagged edges ripping apart all of the important pieces of who Kenneth was. He thought the end had come, that she would finally allow him to bleed and die in peace, but that wasn't in her plan. Filling his personal face, standing almost nose to nose with him, she turned the knife sticking in his stomach just a little more.

"I just wish that when you were signing the papers to kill *my* child, you would have just signed them to kill me too. Then I wouldn't—"

He didn't even feel himself doing it, didn't really know how it actually happened. All he knew was that Heart was pushed against the wall, and his hand was secured around her throat.

He'd only come to realize it was actually his hand around his wife's neck when he felt her nails driving into his skin.

He closed his eyes and beat back the rage threatening to make him cross a line he'd never thought himself capable of, a line he was afraid he was too quickly approaching.

"You are so fortunate that being a wife beater isn't my thing. If it were, you would be in danger of swallowing your tongue. This bullshit ends now. I'm not losing my wife, not after everything else I've lost. You can hurl whatever dirt you want at me, but you will never utter those words again. I did not kill our child. And I will not let you kill us."

~

*H*er brain fought through the building fogginess that seemed to get thicker with each of her labored breaths. Was he really squeezing hard enough to restrict her airflow? No, more likely it was due to the heaving panicked breaths she was taking through her mouth.

She saw his lips begin to move. He was speaking, she needed to focus, whatever he was saying could determine whether they both survived this incident or not. Because if he harmed her the NYPD and her family would hunt him down to the gates of hell and she couldn't allow that to happen.

She'd done this; she'd made him this thing that was holding her so harshly. She couldn't let him suffer another loss. She'd taken so much from him; she'd not take the freedom, the life, and soul he would surely lose if he brought physical harm to her. "Kenneth...please... don't," she mouthed.

"What was that?" Kenneth said as he pressed closer. "You're still trying to control this situation, Heart? When are you going to get it? Your life is quite literally in my hands."

She tried to take another breath, hoping to talk him down, but he shook his head and made a soft shushing sound.

"I've listened too long to what you've had to say. No, today, we're going to do things a little differently. I'm going to talk and you're going to listen. You will never disrespect me like that again. You will never take my kindness as a sign of weakness again. You will learn that just because I don't go around thumping my chest and beating the shit out of you every chance I get doesn't mean that I am to be fucked with. I'm a lot of things, Heart. But weak has never been one of them. You'd do best to remember that shit.

"I've spent the last fourteen weeks in a hell I couldn't have imagined if I'd tried, because you forced me to make a decision that you knew would destroy us. I had my world ripped out from under me, everything taken from me all because things had to be your way or no way. Well

I've lost everything, Heart, but the one thing I'm not about to lose is you."

He snatched his hand away from her neck just as quickly as he'd placed it there in the first place and turned to walk to the opposite wall. As soon as he'd released her she felt her legs give and her back slide down the wall until she was seated on the floor.

She took a shaky hand to her neck and allowed her fingers to quickly run across sweat-laden skin. She was fine, she'd be fine, but Kenneth...

She watched him rake hard, angry fingers through the dark waves of silky black hair. Her fingers twitched a bit, they ached to feel those soft tresses caressing aching skin. She wanted to go to him, hold him, make things right the way she should have three months ago, but she knew it was too late, nothing she did would fix the hurt that she'd heaped on his broad shoulders.

"This bullshit with you running behind these fucking emotional mountains you've erected, hiding from me, that shit ends now. I am your husband, and there isn't an inch of this Earth I wouldn't cross to get to you. You can be mad with me, but the one thing you will never do is end us, Heart. The sooner you figure that shit out, the better off we'll both be. Like it or not...You.

Are. Mine."

She might not have liked what he was saying. She damn sure hadn't liked the way he'd expressed it, but she knew one thing...he was right, she did belong to him.

~

*H*e left; the gentle tick of the bedroom told her that. She went to stand up, but the pain sitting in the middle of her chest, closing off her ability to breathe wouldn't let her up from that spot.

She blinked her eyes, her vision blurred with tears that she'd held so tightly inside for all these months. Every time she attempted to clear her vision, a flash of memory would pass her eyes, like she was watching a television reel of her own life.

The first was a shot of the two of them in her office when they'd first met. The next, the first time he'd ever kissed her. Then she recognized the dingy elevator she'd collapsed in after being shot, she'd never touched the floor because he'd caught her, protected her when she was hurt, sick, weak.

She remembered them walking into this house, getting her the help she needed to heal her emotional and physical wounds. She recalled the first time they'd made love, the fire he'd built and smothered with knowing hands. She remembered the love she'd felt when he'd proposed, and the happiness they shared when they exchanged vows. She knew how each of these memories played out, but watching them bleed one into another ripped at the careful patchwork of the damn she'd cemented in place.

Then she remembered the night she'd told him she was pregnant, she remembered the relief she'd felt at his happiness, how complete it felt to be surrounded in his arms, knowing he would never let any harm come to her and their child.

Their child, their precious innocent baby was gone. Their child never had the chance to survive, its demise determined by a mere accident of nature.

Accident. It was an accident; there was nothing he could have done.

The vice around her chest broke and she took a tentative lungful of air. When the pain didn't follow, she sucked in greedy breaths each clearing more of the emotional fog she'd been living under for so long.

Yes, her baby was gone, but her husband was still here. Or at least he was until she'd tried to push him away.

Pins and needles began to set in, telling her she'd been crouched down on the floor too long. How long she'd been there, she wasn't really certain, but she knew it was time to pull herself out of the emotional filth she'd been wallowing in for so long.

She took short steps until the circulation returned to her feet. She made quick steps down the stairs and walked into the living room.

"Kenneth?"

Her voice echoed off the walls, the silence of the house screaming Kenneth's absence. She went to the basement entrance and opened the door. The light leading downstairs was off. She closed the door and continued on into the kitchen. One click of the light told her what she'd already known. He wasn't in the house.

She looked over to the key hook by the backdoor. His ring was gone, he was gone.

Heart flopped into a chair at the table chewing on her bottom lip. A folded piece of paper with her name on it scribbled in Kenneth's bold block handwriting hooked her gaze.

She sat up quickly, knocking over the peppershaker as she reached for it. Shaky hands held it open as she fought to focus her vision on the words on the page.

Heart,

I love you, and I meant what I said about us working through this.

But right now, I just need to think. Kenneth

Heart dropped the note and slid further into the hard chair. Despite his love for her, she'd still managed to drive her husband away.

A new batch of tears crept up and spilled from closed eyes.

What the fuck have I done?

EPILOGUE

*H*eart stood at the table, looking down at the little folded cards that displayed guests' seating order. There in the middle, she found the card she was looking for.

Mr. & Cap. Searlington Table 2

She picked up the card and fondled it gently. There hadn't been a Mr. and Captain

Searlington for some time now. Their names on this place card were the closest they'd come to being together in nearly a month.

The sad realization that she hadn't seen or spoken to Kenneth in so long made the stone in the pit of her stomach roll wildly. If it didn't hurt so much, she'd almost laugh at the current state of affairs in her life. For months she'd done everything to lock Kenneth out, to drown in her grief alone. Now that she had that... Hindsight really was twenty-twenty.

"MacKenzie." The familiar voice of her former captain pulled her attention away from the card burning in the palm of her hand.

"Hey, Captain," she answered. It didn't matter that the man had been retired for two years, he was still her captain.

"How are you?"

How did she answer that? She was physically fine, functioning on sheer rote memory. But inside, inside she was empty, aching with cold.

She managed a weak smile. "I'm good."

Porter gave her his signature, "I don't believe that bullshit," look and stepped closer to her, looking around once to make certain no one was in ear shot of their conversation.

"He's coming back, you know that don't you? He just needed a little time to decompress."

She nodded her head, yeah, his note had said he wanted to work things out, but in four weeks the only communication she had from him was a weekly text saying he was all right and still working some things out.

She wasn't angry, not at Kenneth anyway. No, the only person she was angry with about this entire situation was herself. She'd pushed her husband away, and she would have to deal with the consequences of those actions.

"Is Aunt Pam with you?" she asked, hoping to pull him off the subject of her broken marriage.

"No, she's visiting out west with our son and his family."

"So it seems like we're both going stag tonight. Wanna sit together?"

He extended his arm to her and she took the anchor gratefully. Walking into a room full of politicians and NYPD brass didn't bode well for the uneasiness that plagued her consistently since she'd pushed Kenneth out the door.

She needed someone to lean on; she'd finally figured that out all too late. If she'd understood that from the beginning, she might have been able to share her grief with her husband instead of using it to push him away.

Lessons learned.

She and Porter took their seats inside the ballroom. Heart's eyes roamed over the sea of navy blue dress uniforms that filled the room, her uniform adding to the spill of indigo that dominated the space.

She pulled at her collar like an antsy child fidgeting in her church clothes. If Kenneth were here, he'd be laughing at her. As much as she loathed this outfit, he'd always worn this glow, a perfect mixture of pride, love, and lust. What she wouldn't give to have him watch her in the confining garments again.

The governor walked on to the dais and gave the welcome address, quickly beginning the ceremony. She clapped, smiled, and cheered in all the appropriate places. She ate the food offered, and made polite conversation with the other guests at the table. She did everything she was supposed to, but she felt absolutely nothing.

The governor took to the stage once again addressing the crowd. She tried to listen, but every sound was muffled through the fog of in her mind. She felt Porter nudge her shoulder.

"MacKenzie, they just called you up there."

She blinked away the murkiness and stood slowly. She made her way to the side of the stage and carefully took each step. The governor grabbed her extended hand and whispered what must have been a "congratulations" in her ear. The commissioner stepped in front of her and she gave him a practiced salute. He returned it and handed her a glass-like plaque, and pointed toward the microphone.

They'd made her dress like a monkey in this damn dress uniform, and now she had to stand up here in front of a room full of people and speak. It was too bad the only thing she really wanted to do was peel this damn uniform off and crawl in the middle of her overly large bed and ache from the loneliness of what seemed to be her unending solitude.

She stepped up to the mic and looked out into the expectant faces of the audience. They were smiling, celebrating the honor that was being bestowed on her and all she could do was seal her eyes to try to keep from crying.

I'm such a fraud.

She read the inscription on the award to the audience.

"Captain Heart Searlington, for your valor, bravery, and dedication to the NYPD and the people of the city of New York. Wow, I almost expect to read someone else's name on this when

I read all of that."

The crowd laughed and she used the reprieve to give herself another moment to quell the fear slipping across her skin.

"I'm very grateful to be chosen for this wonderful honorarium. When I decided to join the NYPD, I did it because I wanted to help the people in my neighborhood. I wanted to protect their freedoms and rights from those that would encroach upon them. Bravery and courage never entered into my mind, I just wanted to help and protect wherever I could.

"Often times people think that when you put yourself in harm's way to protect those who cannot or will not protect themselves that you have no fear. That is the furthest thing from the truth. I've heard it said that courage doesn't mean you aren't afraid, it just means you do what needs to be done despite being afraid.

"Most people in law enforcement will never let you know it, but most of the time; we operate from a place of fear. We're afraid we're not going to be quick enough or strong enough to protect those we are charged with, while at the same time fearing we might not be able to protect ourselves.

"My gun and my badge have never made me feel safe; they've always made me keenly aware of how fragile life, all life, really is. How precious it really is.

"The only time people of law enforcement feel safe is when they are in the arms of their loved ones, the people that keep our homes warm and fill our hearts with love. If I am able to perform brave acts, it's because there was someone at home making me feel safe and protected.

A feeling I never truly experienced before I met my husband, Kenneth Searlington."

The crowd clapped, she could see people looking around, as if they were trying to find him in the audience.

"Kenneth couldn't be here tonight, but in his absence, I wanted to dedicate this award to him. Kenneth, it is only because of the love, courage, and confidence that you've poured into my life throughout the course of our relationship that I am able to discharge my duties. The late nights you waited up for me, the encouragement, the support, the love, the understanding, it all makes me the officer that stands here today. Know that there will never come a day when I don't want your brand of love in my life."

The room filled with thunderous applause as audience members stood on their feet and cheered for Heart. She should have been filled with such joy to witness this kind of reception. Unfortunately, sadness had a way of bleeding her world of any joy lately, so she hid her pain behind a false smile and headed for the door.

Heart waited for the valet to bring her car around when she felt an electric buzz humming along her skin and spine and she wanted to turn around to seek out the cause of it, but she feared her worn-raw emotions were playing tricks on her mind.

"Did you mean it?"

She shivered; it felt so much longer than just the four weeks since she'd last heard it. It was familiar, warm, not hard and angry like the last time.

"Mean what?"

She felt his warmth paint her back, burning through the material of her uniform jacket. God how she'd missed that feeling, that heat that permeated through all her layers, bringing life to the chilled spots that lived inside of her.

"The part of your speech where you said you'd never want to live without my love."

She felt the pads of his fingers trace the backside of her hand. It traveled down the knuckle of her marriage finger over the bumps of the diamonds in her wedding rings.

"Yeah," she nodded, "I did."

He was standing beside her now; he moved his hand up her sleeved arm, turning her by her shoulder, forcing her to rest her eyes on him. Her heart hurt. The sight of him after living with his absence was painful. Her thirsty soul was so eager to drink him in.

"Good, because the feeling's mutual. I don't plan to live without your love either. You do know that don't you?"

"I tried to remember that, Kenneth," she answered. "But I can't lie and say that your absence didn't disturb me, worry me. I understood it though. I understand that I made things too intense for you. The things I said to you…"

"Heart, I didn't leave because of what you said to me. To hear you accuse me of killing our unborn child killed something inside me. It broke me, but it never made me not want to be with you. I understood it was coming from a place of grief. I understood that the pain you were in was messing with your head."

"Then why did you go?"

The valet arrived with her car at that moment. Kenneth took the keys from him and opened

Heart's door for her, bidding her to take the passenger seat. He pulled out into traffic easily, and maneuvered them toward the highway.

With minimal traffic, they were walking through the doors of their home in a short amount of time. Heart removed her layers, unbuttoned her sleeves, cuffing them until they reached the middle of her forearms. Next, she pulled her tie off and unhooked the first button.

Heaven.

She hated that fucking uniform. She looked up to find Kenneth smiling at her. His eyes were filled with laughter and tinged with a small bit of lust.

"I've missed seeing you in that thing," he beamed.

"Yeah, I know how the police uniform does it for you."

"No, you in a police uniform does it for me," he laughed. "Heart, everything about you does it for me."

"Then why did you leave, and where did you go?"

"I went to my London office; I just needed to be somewhere that I couldn't come running back to you whenever I wanted. Somewhere I would be forced to examine myself."

"But why?" she asked.

"Heart, that night I let my rage get way out of control. I have been angry before, but I never felt that out of control. I put my hands on you, Heart."

She lifted up her hand to stop him. "Kenneth, you did not hurt me, you did not hit me."

"But I could have. I was angry enough that I could have, and that scared the shit out of me. I needed to check myself for a bit, make certain I wasn't turning in to the ugly monster I felt like. I would never have survived hurting you."

She walked over to him and directed him toward the couch. When seated, she grabbed his hand and laced her fingers through his.

"Kenneth, I was dead ass wrong. But even though I was, you still didn't use that as an excuse to turn into an abusive asshole. You walked away. You did what you were supposed to.

What we both needed you to do. I'm ashamed to admit it, but it wasn't until you were gone that I realized what I'd done, what I'd put in jeopardy. I should never have robbed you of your grief."

He nodded. "I'll admit that was the hardest part. Not being able to mourn our child with you…I felt like I was drowning."

"Kenneth, I don't fault you for any of this. You tried to reach me, but I just felt too guilty to let you in."

"Guilty?" he asked.

"Kenneth, I don't think I realized it then, but part of my resentment was based solely on the fact that I needed someone else to blame for something I believed myself responsible for. I didn't even think about the baby when I went after that fool in the bodega. It never occurred to me that this might not be something that a pregnant woman should be doing. I just fell back into training, and completely forgot what I was risking.

"I know that the pregnancy never would have survived, even if I hadn't apprehended a criminal. I know that, but inside…it just felt… feels like it was my fault. Blaming you was the only way I could live with myself. I'm so sorry, Kenneth."

He reached for her; let warm hands melt against her skin. There was a moment of hesitation in his eyes, then he placed smooth lips on hers and she felt the pieces begin to click in place. He tasted her, more like savored her mouth. Smooth slow strokes of his tongue made her lace covered nipples tighten pressing painfully against the thin material.

"Fuck this," the rough words falling from her lips made him break their connection.

She used the momentum to push him back on the couch. She ripped the buttons of his shirt, a satisfied smile climbing her lips as each button pinged off of the surfaces surrounding them.

"Shit, Heart, that's a fucking designer tuxedo shirt. You couldn't have asked me to take it off?"

"Where would the fun be in that," she answered.

There was a spark of fire in the deep blue of his eyes. "Yeah, you're right." He stood up and returned the favor, ripping the sides of her shirt apart.

There was a look of reverence on his face. He stepped closer to her, letting shaky fingers walk down the front of her chest.

"I've missed you so much," he whispered.

"Then show me."

He made little work of getting them both naked then gently laid her on the floor. He dipped his fingers inside her pussy and that hungry bitch swallowed like a thirsty man in the dessert.

"God you're so wet already?"

"Yes, so shut up and get on with it," she answered through gritted teeth.

He must have realized how serious she was because she felt him pressed to her entrance. Kenneth was king of fucking foreplay, a fact she usually loved. But it had been four months since the last time they'd made love, and if he didn't fuck her right now she was liable to break him. Hell, even if he did fuck her, he wasn't walking away from this meeting unscathed. He joined them in one brutal thrust that caused both of them to cry out.

"Fuck, woman, you're gonna kill me."

She locked her fingers in his glorious strands and yanked him down to her mouth.

"That's the plan."

They were fire together, burning embers smoldering, clouding the air with the scent of their sex. She could already feel the climax building from the inhuman pace of him slamming into that perfect fucking spot over and over again. One, two more strokes and she was carving the skin of his ass cheeks with her nails and screaming his name. She felt him falter, his strokes beating out a staccato rhythm that was pulling her orgasm out of her. Hard fingers bit into the flesh of her thigh and teeth marred the skin on her shoulder when his muscles locked and she felt the first stream of his cum coat her walls.

They remained there, tied together through body and love. The way they were always meant to be.

"We can never have a divided heart again," he mumbled.

"What?"

"You me, we were always meant to be one heart. From that very first day two years ago, we were always supposed to be one heart. When we're separated, when we're not on the same page, we split that heart, weaken it. We're stronger together, so never again can we live with a divided heart."

She smiled and raised an achy limb to his face and playfully mushed him. "You say the sappiest shit sometimes."

"Yeah, I do, but you still love me anyway."

Her smile widened and happiness filled her up, pressing against the seams of her heart.

"Indeed I do, Mr. Searlington, indeed I do."

The End

ABOUT THE AUTHOR

LaQuette is an erotic, multicultural romance author of M/F and M/M love stories. Her writing style brings intellect to the drama. She often crafts emotionally epic, fantastical tales that are deeply pigmented by reality's paintbrush. Her novels are filled with a unique mixture of savvy, sarcastic, brazen, and unapologetically sexy characters who are confident in their right to appear on the page.

This bestselling Erotic Romance Author is the 2016 Author of the Year Golden Apple Award Winner, 2016 Write Touch Award Winner for Best Contemporary Mid-length Novel, 2016 Swirl Awards 1st Place Winner in Romantic Suspense, and 2016 Aspen Gold Award Finalist in Erotic Romance. LaQuette—a native of Brooklyn, New York—spends her time catering to her three distinct personalities: Wife, Mother, and Educator.

Writing—her escape from everyday madness—has always been a friend and source of comfort. At the age of sixteen she read her first romance novel and realized the genre was missing something: people who looked and lived like her. As a result, her characters and settings are always designed to provide positive representations of people of color and various marginalized communities.

She loves hearing from readers and discussing the crazy characters that are running around in her head causing so much trouble. Contact her on:

Website: www.LaQuette.com
Email: LaQuette@LaQuette.com
Amazon: www.amazon.com/author/laquette
Facebook: www.facebook.com/LaQuetteTheAuthor
Twitter: www.twitter.com/LaQuetteWrites
Instagram: www.instagram.com/la_quette

OTHER TITLES

Wicked Wager: Texas vs. Brooklyn 1
Bedding The Enemy
Lies You Tell
Heart of the Matter: Queens of Kings: Book 1
Divided Heart: Queens of Kings: Book 2
Protected Heart: Queens of Kings Book 3
Power Privilege & Pleasure: Queens of Kings: Book 4
His True Strength: Queens of Kings: Book 5
Love's Changes: A Losing My Way Novella
My Beginning: Trinity Series: Book 1

NEWSLETTER SIGNUP

Hello,

If you're interested in staying current with all the happenings with my writing, previews, and giveaways, sign up for my monthly newsletter at www.LaQuette.com.

Keep it sexy,
LaQuette 💋

COMING SOON...

LOADED LONGSHOT

Texas vs. Brooklyn 2

Kandi Adkins, the executive manager of Sweet Sadie's Cosmetics, has her roots planted firmly in Brownsville, Brooklyn. Kandi knows what it's like to have nothing. Education and her friend's late mother, Sadie King, pulled her out of the mire of poverty and enabled her to grab hold to personal and professional security.

Life has taught Aaron Nakai to play his cards close to the vest. Reaching for more than you need only invites trouble into your life. That's what happened to his father, a man who died young attempting to make his mark on the world. He finds comfort and security living in his adoptive brother, Slade's, shadow. Aaron refuses to allow lofty dreams to rob him of the gains he made in life. Being Slade's lawyer and right-hand man suits him just fine.

When Slade needs Aaron to step out of the background and take care of an unexpected problem in New York, Aaron's quiet existence back in Texas is blown to bits by a quick-witted, sassy-mouthed fireball named Kandi. Their attraction is just as palpable as their distaste for one another, making the decision to wager their hearts and their careers a high-stakes game with potentially disastrous outcomes.

Will they fold? Or will they reach for a loaded longshot to win it all?

COMING SOON...

SEDUCTIVE STAKES

Texas vs. Brooklyn 3

Azure Carlisle is simply tired. She's tired of always struggling to do the right thing only to have life slap her down time and time again. She climbed her way out of the projects of Brooklyn by getting an education. Her Ph.D. in Chemistry was her ticket out of the 'hood, but the lingering student loans from both her undergraduate and graduate degrees crush any dreams of personal advancement.

When the financial juggling game she plays every month begins to topple, Azure stumbles upon a way out. With an offer to clear her debts in hand, Azure is nearly burden free. The only thing she must do to escape financial ruin is simple: betray the trust of the woman who offered her a job, and friendship.

Damien Mesías is the former CEO of Logan Industries. He's spent his life paying for the sin of his father's illegitimacy. When your dad is the result of a salacious affair between the respectably married tycoon and his maid, you're not as welcome to the family gatherings as your legitimate cousins.

Determined to prove his worth, and exact his revenge against the remaining Logan heir, his cousin, Slade Hamilton, Damien embarked on a dangerous path that nearly ruined him and the family business. Destroyed, divorced, and wallowing in a pit of despair, Damien aches for peace and forgiveness. But, with so much to atone for, those two things are elusive goals Damien isn't quite sure he can attain.

When an opportunity to get into Slade's good graces appears, Damien rushes to Brooklyn and finds his job is more complicated than he believed. One, the thief is a friend of the family, and two, she's the sexiest thing Damien has seen in a long time. Torn between his desire to do the right thing, and his need to have Azure, Damien is forced to make a decision that could destroy them all.

Will Damien ruin friendships, and Azure's life, by exposing her? Will Azure sell-out the people who have supported her to gain financial freedom? Or, will Damien's wild card play present seductive stakes that neither of them can walk away from?

www.ingramcontent.com/pod-product-compliance
Lightning Source LLC
Chambersburg PA
CBHW031421250626
47155CB00004B/1575